CODENAME **QUICKSILVER**

The Tyrant King

Look out for the other
CODENAME **QUICKSILVER** books

In the Zone

Burning Sky

Killchase

Adrenaline Rush

End Game

CODENAME
QUICKSILVER

The Tyrant King

Allan Jones

Orion
Children's Books

With special thanks to Rob Rudderham

First published in Great Britain in 2012
by Orion Children's Books
a division of the Orion Publishing Group Ltd
Orion House
5 Upper St Martin's Lane
London WC2H 9EA
An Hachette UK company

3 5 7 9 10 8 6 4 2

The Orion Publishing Group's policy is to use papers that are natural, renewable and recyclable products and made from wood grown in sustainable forests. The logging and manufacturing processes are expected to conform to the environmental regulations of the country of origin.

A catalogue record for this book is available from the British Library.

ISBN 978 1 4440 0546 2

Printed in Great Britain by Clays Ltd, St Ives plc

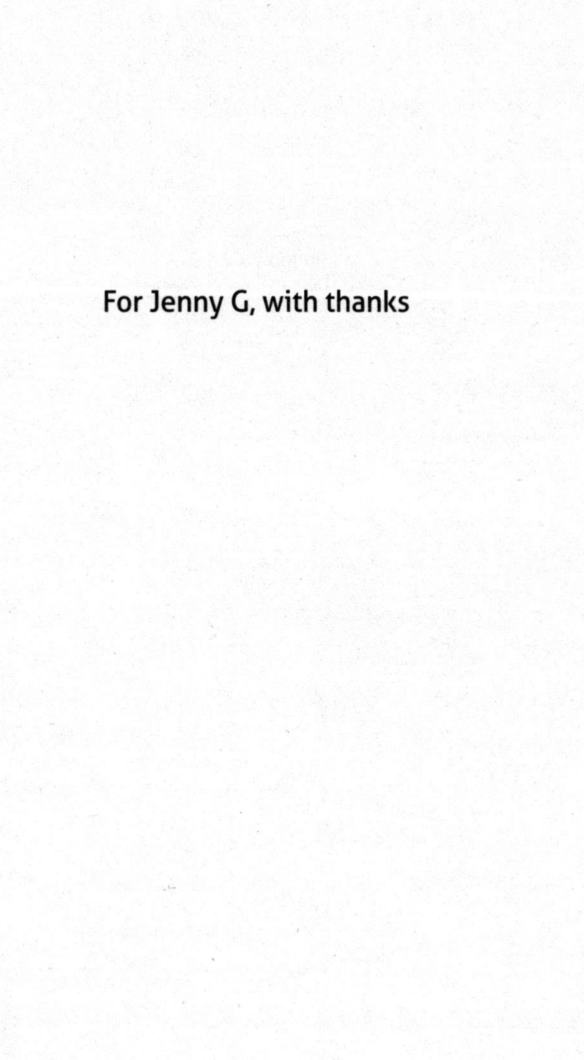

For Jenny G, with thanks

CHAPTER **ONE**

Zak Archer was in the zone. Alert. Tireless. Wired.

He had never felt so alive in his life. Which was odd, considering how many people were out to get him.

Dawn had just broken. He was on the outskirts of the town. He had almost reached his objective.

Almost.

He dived for cover then belly crawled to a low wall, his backpack bouncing on his shoulders.

He crouched behind the wall and checked his Mob.

Things looked good.

So far.

The Mob was a smartphone used by British Intelligence. It was slim, oval and silvery, with an 80GB capacity. Cutting-edge technology. Zak pinched and flicked and the on-screen map expanded, showing the town in more detail.

A blue pulse showed his position. A red dot revealed his target. A yellow line ran along the shortest route between the two points.

Zak tried to stay calm and focused, but his heart was beating fast. It was a cool, overcast morning, but sweat was running down his forehead.

This was all happening too soon. He wasn't ready for it. Colonel Hunter had made a big mistake asking him to undertake this mission. He'd fail – and that would be it.

Done. Finished.

No! Stop thinking like that.

He pulled off his backpack and opened it. He took out the snakescope, a nifty gadget which looked like a conical pair of binoculars with a flexible cable attached to the front. Great for seeing around corners.

He kneeled and fed the cable over the top of the wall, twisting the dials as he looked through the twin eyepieces. A magnified circle roved across the deserted streets.

No sign of life. But it was creepy to know that there

were enemies hidden somewhere out there, waiting for the opportunity to get the drop on him.

Zak had undergone eleven weeks of intensive physical training since joining Project 17's fast-track course. It had been gruelling and relentless, and there were plenty of nights when he'd crashed out in his bunk bed, aching in places he never knew existed.

And now he had to make use of every trick he'd learned, or Project 17 would be down one agent and his new life would be over as soon as it had started.

No pressure, then.

He turned and put the snakescope into his backpack. Fitting the pack over his shoulders, he leaned against the wall. He closed his eyes and focused on his breathing.

Go on four.

One . . . two . . . three . . . GO!

He darted up and over the wall, running hard, arms pumping, feet skimming the tarmac. Part of his training had been about learning to control his ability to get into the zone.

The zone.

The zone had always been there, although it had never had a name till he'd met the young agents who formed the branch of British Secret Services called Project 17.

The zone was a place where the gears between his brain and his muscles meshed. The zone was a place where he could outrun the wind. The zone was the best place in the world.

Zak heard the whine of a bullet and the sharp skip as it ricocheted off the ground at his heels.

They had found him.

Even in the zone, he couldn't outrun a sniper's bullet.

He looked around, seeking new cover.

A window was open – no more than thirty centimetres – but it was enough. He bounded over a low stone wall, across soft earth and, arms pointed like a diver's, through the narrow gap.

He rolled across bare floorboards, limbs tucked in, head down, letting his momentum carry him to the far wall.

Then he sprang up, listening for movement over the hammering of the blood in his temples.

Booted feet. Running fast. Coming closer.

He was out of the door and halfway up a staircase almost before his brain could catch up with him. He raced along a hallway to a back room, pulled the window open and peered down. There was the sloping roof of an outhouse beneath him, then a bare stretch of earth, a fence, and another row of houses.

Zak jumped onto the windowsill and let himself drop, sliding down the roof. He caught the gutter with both hands, boosted himself off, then somersaulted onto hard-packed earth and started running again the moment his feet hit. Up and over the fence and into a narrow alley.

That was when he heard the distant throb of helicopter rotors.

Wow. They really were throwing everything at him.

A black Humvee skidded to a roaring halt at the end of the alley. Blocking his way out.

Zak knew he was almost out of options. But not quite. He ran towards the vehicle, gathering speed, his mind sharp.

He launched himself into the air, kicking out so his feet struck the car door just as it was being opened. There was a yell as the door crashed shut. His momentum lifted him. He landed with both feet on the roof of the Humvee, then sprang forwards, hitting the ground shoulder first. Rolling. On his feet again and heading away at top speed.

He heard shouting. A bullet zinged, striking sparks off a raised walkway directly ahead.

He snatched at the metal railings and slid through on a cushion of air. Rolling across paving stones. Up again. Running across an open courtyard between tall buildings. People in black were coming at him from all sides now. Five or six of them, only eyes and mouths visible through black masks.

Zak jumped onto the top of the first of a row of concrete bollards, then bounced from one to another along the whole row as his pursuers tried in vain to grab him out of the air.

No chance!

He sprang from the top of the last bollard, using every ounce of muscle power to boost himself up onto a high wall. He snatched at the top, his feet striking the brickwork, propelling him up and over onto a flat tarred roof.

He raced to another wall and scaled it at speed. But he was running against the skyline now – an easy target. And he could see the black helicopter gliding towards him like a high-tech mosquito.

He had to get off that roof and quickly.

He jumped again, aiming for the wall of an adjacent building. He flexed his legs and bounced backwards and forwards between the walls of the two buildings as he plummeted to the ground.

He landed well, absorbing the impact with bent knees, and continued down the long alley.

Zak took out his Mob and flicked to find the map again.

The blue pulse and the red dot were nearly touching. He had almost hit the target.

Now speed would have to give way to stealth.

He dipped into his backpack and pulled out a Taz – an electronic device designed to deliver an electric shock. It looked like a slim black torch. He flicked a switch and a red spot lit up.

The Taz was fully charged.

He edged along the wall and shot a glance around the corner. There was a single guard at the door.

Zak moved closer, silent as a ghost.

It was no good. The man heard him. He turned, raising his automatic machine gun, eyes fierce through the black ski mask.

Nothing to lose now.

Zak hurled himself forwards, gripping the Taz like a knife. He cannoned into the man, aiming the Taz at the man's neck as they both tumbled to the ground.

But he missed his mark. The man was twice his size and weight. He threw Zak off easily and sent him flying so that he landed in a dizzy heap.

He rolled onto his back and saw the man looming over him, silhouetted against the white sky.

"Not this time, kid," he said, aiming the gun.

Zak flung out his arm, flicking the switch on the handle of the Taz. A pair of micro-wires snaked out, the twin barbed electrodes digging into the man's thigh. The Taz hummed and vibrated with power as the man collapsed on the ground.

Then Zak was on his feet. He pulled the gun from the man's hands and threw it aside. The man would be up again the moment the electric charge ran out. He had only a few seconds.

He raced up the steps to the entrance of the target building. It was an office block. He ran into a wide, empty foyer.

He saw the thin tripwire a thousandth of a second before his ankle hit it. He stumbled to a halt as the wire snapped.

"Oh, no! *No!*"

There was a loud muffled bang and suddenly the foyer was full of billowing grey smoke. Zak felt the floor fall away beneath his feet.

He went crashing down into darkness.

So close, and right at the end he'd walked into a booby trap.

Idiot!

He landed heavily, and lay gasping as the smoke swirled around him.

A figure emerged at his side. A heavy boot pressed down on his chest.

Eyes glinted through a ski mask. A machine pistol pointed at him.

"Game over," said a voice.

There was a sharp crack and Zak felt an intense pain in his chest.

CHAPTER **TWO**

"Get off me!" Zak groaned.

The figure lifted its foot and pulled the mask away to reveal a wide, high-cheek-boned face under slicked-down hair. Agent Jackhammer shouldered his paint gun and reached a hand down to Zak, hauling him to his feet.

Zak rubbed his chest. His fingers were smeared with red paint.

"That hurt," he said. "Aren't you meant to shoot from at least three metres away?"

Jackhammer grinned and nodded.

Zak heard applause from above. He looked up. The

smoke was clearing. A group of people in black were standing around the trapdoor through which he'd fallen.

"Well done, Agent Quicksilver," Colonel Hunter called. The applause rose and there were a few whistles and whoops.

"Way to go, Silver!" he heard Switchblade shout. "You almost made it all the way."

Zak smiled despite the ache in his chest.

Jackhammer turned and walked outside. Zak followed.

By the time he emerged into the open, the helicopter was gone and the SAS soldiers were already piling into their vehicles. Their commander shook Colonel Hunter's hand as the last of them climbed into the armoured personnel carrier. The engine gunned, and there was a screech of rubber as the army vehicle sped along the deserted road.

"Did I pass?" Zak asked the Colonel.

"I'll make a full assessment of your performance in the next few days," the Colonel replied. "But I don't think you have anything to worry about." He turned away, speaking rapidly into his Mob.

Zak grinned. He thought he'd blown it when he hit the tripwire. But he was in! He'd passed Project 17's physical training course. He was on his way to becoming a full agent. The others gathered around him.

Jackhammer slapped Zak on the back, almost knocking him over. "Not bad, kid," he said. "We might make an agent of you yet."

Switch lassoed Zak's neck with his arm and knuckled his head playfully. "You did good, Silver!" he said. "I only got to the plaza when I took the Run. That thing with the bollards – amazing!"

Zak grinned, wriggling free of Switchblade's over-enthusiastic grip.

"It's no big deal," he said jokingly. "I do what I do, you know?"

Colonel Hunter's voice rang out. "We're off, people. Leave the place the way you'd like to find it." He approached Zak. "You'll be dropped off at the Academy," he told him. "Switchblade, Wildcat and Jackhammer – you're in the van with him. After the drop off, head for London. We'll meet at Fortress at seventeen hundred."

Two black transit vans pulled up and the agents of Project 17 scrambled inside. Zak sat in the back with Jackhammer and Switchblade and a female agent called Wildcat. She was a strange one, Zak thought. She spent all her free time working out in the gym or playing brain-fryingly complicated logic games on her Mob. She had an explosion of ash-white hair and she wore black lipstick and thick black eyeliner.

A Goth secret agent. That was new!

Zak looked out of the tinted windows of the van as they drove away from the town and up into the hills.

It wasn't a real town at all – it had been built by the British Army to train for urban warfare. No one had ever lived there. No one ever would. It sat in a remote valley in the countryside and hardly anyone even knew it existed.

"I knew I'd lost it when I hit that tripwire," Zak said. He was still buzzing from the adrenaline rush of the chase. "Has anyone ever got in and out with the information?"

Jackhammer shook his head. "Hardly anyone even gets into the building." Zak liked the new note of respect in his voice. Hammer was hard to impress. "I heard of one guy who got right into the target room before they took him down," he continued, "but that was only once, if it happened at all."

"It was four years ago," Wildcat said. "The guy was codename Slingshot. But he wasn't in Project 17 – he was in another branch of the Secret Services. Everyone in MI5 training has to do the Run at some point." The others looked at her. "What? I read the files in the computer archives," she said. "I like to read."

Zak realized it was crazy, but knowing that just *one* MI5 agent had done better than him on the Run made his competitive hackles rise. Who was this Slingshot, and what was so special about him?

"I've never heard of Slingshot," said Switch. "What happened to him?"

Wildcat shrugged and went back to her Mob. "No idea," she said casually. "Discontinued, maybe."

Zak shivered. He didn't know why. His friend Dodge would have said: "Someone just walked on your grave, Zachary." Not a nice feeling.

Discontinued. What did that mean? Quit? Dead? Zak found he really wanted to know.

The van bounced along the rough track, jolting and jarring its passengers as it crossed the empty hills. Zak leaned his head against the side of the van, thinking about his curious friendship with Dodge – the homeless man who lived under the arches of Waterloo station in London.

Dodge was his one true adult friend. It had all started with the sharing of a cheese sandwich. Zak had food, Dodge had looked hungry. That had been more than two years ago now – and since then they had been really tight. Dodge would be proud of him right now, Zak thought. He hadn't seen Dodge for weeks, but he was hoping to get away some time soon to tell him about his new life. He'd sworn Dodge to secrecy. Dodge would never say a word about Project 17.

Jackhammer poked Zak in the ribs, jerking him out of his thoughts.

"You think it's been hard work so far?" Hammer said with a grin.

"Yes," said Zak, frowning and pushing his hand away.

"Try sixteen weeks in a classroom," Hammer laughed. "You've got some hardcore brainwork coming up."

Zak already knew that. Before he could become a full agent, he had to undertake a four-month academic course. Desk work. Brain work. What Colonel Hunter called "a steep learning curve".

He'd already had a taste of what was to come. The Colonel had given him a map of London that revealed all the secret tunnels which burrowed under the streets and buildings of the capital. Every tunnel had a code-mark in it, and by learning those codes, a person could move unseen right across subterranean London and always know exactly where they were. It had been a lot to take in, but Zak had a good memory, and he'd cracked most of it already.

"Do you know how many people flunk the Academy?" Switchblade said.

"No, I don't," Zak replied. "But I bet you're dying to tell me."

"One in three," said Switch.

"I won't flunk," Zak said.

Jackhammer laughed. "Easy to say that now."

"You passed, and you've got the brainpower of a gym sock," Zak retorted. "I think I'll be fine."

Jackhammer winked and made a shooting gesture with his finger. Hammer could be okay, as long as you gave as good as you got.

Switchblade's Mob buzzed. He frowned and put it to his ear.

"Yes, Control?"

Zak heard Colonel Hunter's faint voice. He was in the other van, heading to London.

"Got it." There was a sudden urgency to Switchblade's tone. He called to the driver. "Change of plan – Control wants us back at Fortress as quickly as possible."

"What about Quicksilver?" the driver asked.

"He's with us," said Switchblade. He glanced at Zak. "Looks like the Academy is going to have to wait," he said.

The room was very high-tech. White walls. No windows. Lit by halogen strips. A wide plasma screen filled the wall at one end. You wouldn't have known from the inside, but the room was thirty metres below ground level, under

Moorgate station in London, deep in the heart of the secret underground complex known as Fortress.

Zak, Switch, Jackhammer and Wildcat sat facing the screen, waiting for the show to begin. Bug was there too. Bug spent most of his time in his own little room filled with computers and plasma screens and a collection of toy frogs. As far as computers were concerned, twelve-year-old Bug was the uber-nerd, the King of Geeks.

The door opened and Colonel Hunter entered. "Okay, people," he began immediately. "We've been asked to help out with a situation that's developing in Montevisto." He stepped up to the screen. "Bug – light it up."

Bug tapped at a handheld electronic device and the screen burst into life.

It showed a satellite image of a curving coastline above blue sea. The picture zoomed in on the long stretch of a seafront town with forested hills behind.

"This is Montevisto," said the Colonel. "It's a sovereign city state, a self-ruling kingdom on the French Riviera. Bug – show and tell, please."

The satellite image morphed into a map. Zak leaned forwards, taking it all in. Wondering where this briefing was going.

A series of photographs popped up along the top of the screen. A middle-aged man, stern and severe, with a neat-trimmed greying beard. A younger woman, blonde, stunningly beautiful. "The Corvetti family has ruled Montevisto for three hundred years. This is King Edgar III and his wife, Sophia."

"Way to go, Edgar," Jackhammer sang out. "Looks like he hooked himself a supermodel."

"Queen Sophia is twenty years younger than the king," Colonel Hunter continued. "And, yes, well spotted, Jackhammer, she was a photographers' model before she married the king." A third photo appeared – this time of a rather solemn-looking boy with fair hair and wide blue eyes. "They have one son and heir – the Crown Prince Viktor." A fourth picture showed a young man in his late teens – handsome, wearing what looked like motor racing clothes, grinning into the camera. "This is the King's nephew, Prince Rafe, the son of Edgar's younger sister. Prince Rafe's parents were killed five years ago in a terrorist attack."

The word *terrorist*, Zak noticed, suddenly caught everyone's attention.

"What kind of terrorists do they have?" asked Wildcat.

"They're a group calling themselves MARS," said the Colonel. "Their full title is the Montevisto Anti Royalist Strike-force. Their professed aim is to turn Montevisto into a republic – to get rid of the monarchy. But the kind of republic they have in mind would not be democratic. From their manifesto, it's certain that they would set up a very unpleasant totalitarian state." The Colonel gestured to some documents set in front of each agent. "After this briefing, you'll need to read those background files. They give a full account of all the trouble MARS has caused in Montevisto over the past fifteen years, as well as documentation detailing the security measures imposed by the security services to try and stamp them out."

Zak flicked quickly through the papers on the desk. Among the closely typed documents, there were newspaper reports of atrocities, photos of burned out cars and wrecked buildings, and bodies covered with sheets.

"As you can see, MARS has caused a lot of trouble in the past, but they've been almost wiped out inside Montevisto, thanks to the work of the King's security forces," the Colonel continued. "However, they're down but not out. Although they have very few active followers in Montevisto itself, it is believed that they have sleeper cells in cities in various parts of the world – including one right here in London."

"What's a sleeper cell?" Zak asked, guessing he was the only one in the room who didn't know the answer.

"It's a small group of dedicated fanatics who blend into their surroundings," said the Colonel. "They live in ordinary houses, have ordinary jobs. Walk the dog. Go to the local supermarket. The kind of neighbours you'd say hello to if you saw them in the street."

"But underneath, they're sneaky and evil," said Switch. "Underneath it all, they're just waiting for the word. Then they go to work and bad things happen."

"Which is why Project 17 has been asked to become involved." The Colonel's voice took on a steely edge. "In two days' time, King Edgar, Queen Sophia and the two Princes will be coming to London – and we have good reason to believe that a sleeper cell of MARS intends to stage a deadly force attack while they're here." His eyes narrowed. "We believe they plan to kill the King."

CHAPTER **THREE**

The briefing room was silent for a few moments after the Colonel's revelation. The tension and focus of the room had changed somehow. Zak felt it himself – a tightness in his stomach, a tingling sense of danger. All eyes were on Colonel Hunter as he continued the briefing.

"An international summit on climate change is taking place in London this week," he said. "King Edgar is one of the foremost experts in this field, and he'll be giving a keynote speech on the opening day." His eyes flashed as he looked at them all in turn. "This isn't just about saving the monarchy of Montevisto from a group of bad people," he said. "King Edgar will have a vital role to play in any international efforts to combat global warming."

"And we'll be on royal security watch?" asked Jackhammer. "Cool! Way to save the planet!"

"Our mission is not to protect the King himself," said Colonel Hunter. "MI5 have that covered. We've been asked to provide 24/7 cover for Prince Viktor. It's felt that younger agents will be less conspicuous – MI5 don't want to draw too much attention to the mission." He turned to Zak. "This is where you come in, Quicksilver. You're an expert on dinosaurs, yes?"

Zak blinked. Where did that question come from? "I wouldn't say I was an expert, exactly . . ."

The Colonel frowned. "On the form you filled in when you were recruited, you listed among your hobbies an interest in dinosaurs."

"Oh, yes," Zak stammered. It had been a long form – twelve pages of questions. "I'm interested in dinosaurs, of course." He shrugged. "Isn't everyone?"

"Everyone under the age of eight," murmured Jackhammer.

Zak shot him an irritated glance.

"So you do know about them?" insisted the Colonel.

"Well, I can tell a stegosaurus from a diplodocus, if that's what you mean," said Zak.

"And have you heard of a computer game called TR3000?" asked the Colonel.

Zak shook his head.

"Find out about it," said the Colonel. "That's your number-one priority right now. TR3000 is the reason Prince Viktor will be accompanying his parents to London." He turned to the others. "Wildcat, Switchblade – you'll accompany Quicksilver to Montevisto. I'm sending him over to give him a chance to bond with the Prince. I want you two on hand to make sure everything goes smoothly. Start packing – you're all booked on a flight at zero-eight-hundred tomorrow morning." He folded his arms. "You'll receive more details of the mission as soon as they're available. Meanwhile, be smart and be safe. Dismissed."

Zak got up. He felt a little shell shocked at how quickly things were moving. A few minutes ago, all he'd known about Montevisto was that it was a little point on the north-west coast of the Mediterranean Sea. This time tomorrow, he'd be there.

It was six-thirty the next morning. Zak was in his room in another part of the Fortress complex. It wasn't exactly a huge room, but he'd customized it as best he could and it was beginning to feel like home. There was a bed, a small desk with a computer, a cupboard for clothes and some shelves for books and stuff. And there was a private bathroom attached, which came in handy when he turned up filthy and sweaty from a long day's work out.

A canvas holdall was open on the bed, half full of clothes. He also had some other special items Colonel Hunter thought he might need on the mission.

There was a slimline pencil torch, only ten centimetres long, powered by a lithium ion battery and with an amazingly powerful beam. There was a pair of shoes. In the twist-away heel of the right shoe, a thin flexible saw blade was curled up in a hidden compartment. Top spy stuff.

Colonel Hunter had also told him something important, a codeword – only to be used in the most high-risk situations. "The significance of the codeword is universally understood throughout British Intelligence," the Colonel had said. "You never use it unless lives are in imminent danger, got it?"

Zak had nodded. He got it.

The codeword was WINTER.

Zak carried on putting things into the holdall. Once he was packed and ready, he had one errand to run before they left for the airport. A personal errand, although he wasn't at all sure why it mattered to him.

He opened a drawer, pulled out a green and brown beanbag frog and left the room.

"Hi, Bug, how's it going?" Zak stuck his head around the door of Bug's room. "I've got something for you." He held out the beanbag frog and shook it so it rattled and waggled its legs.

Bug smiled and beckoned Zak in.

"He's called King Edgar," Zak said, sitting the frog on the work surface. "If you squeeze him he makes five different kinds of real-life frog calls." He gave Bug a sideways look. "Are you busy?"

Bug pointed to the eight plasma screens lined up on the wall in front of him. The screens showed various scenes of pastel-coloured buildings in bright sunlight – imposing seafront hotels, narrow winding streets, a marina where luxury yachts were moored alongside old fishing boats. And there were villas and busy restaurants and ornate churches, all crowned by a Gothic castle perched high on a cliff under a crystal blue sky.

"Is that Montevisto?" asked Zak.

Bug nodded. "The pictures are patched through from

the local CCTV network," he said. "I've dug up all the info I can find on TR3000. I'm going to download it to your Mob – you can check it out on the aeroplane. It looks amazing. If the publicity is genuine, then it's going to be the biggest leap forward in virtual reality computer games in the last decade."

"Great," said Zak. "Hey, I was wondering whether you could look something up for me. Something else."

Bug's dark eyes peered enquiringly at Zak from under his fringe.

"There used to be a guy in MI5 called Slingshot," Zak said. "Can you find out about him for me?" Zak still wasn't really sure why he wanted to know more about the mysterious MI5 agent. Was it that Slingshot was the only agent who'd done better in the Run than he had? Or was it something else? Whatever it was, he was intrigued, and surely it couldn't hurt just to delve a bit deeper.

Bug tapped at his keyboard. One of the screens changed to an official home page.

Password Protected.

Bug tapped again and a new page opened. He scrolled down while Zak leaned over his shoulder. Bug came to a search option and typed in Slingshot.

An insert popped up.

Codename Slingshot.

All information has been archived and is Firewalled with Alpha Clearance Access only.

"What does that mean?" asked Zak.

"It means you'd need to have a way higher clearance code than me to be allowed to read the file," Bug said.

"That's weird," Zak replied. "Wildcat said she'd read this recently."

Bug nodded. "Could be," he said. "The new clearance code was only implemented a few weeks ago."

Zak frowned. "How many weeks?"

Bug typed and a sub-page opened, displaying a long list of letters and numbers and symbols. "Colonel Hunter posted the new clearance code eleven weeks ago," Bug said. He turned to look at Zak. "Interesting," he added. "He did it the same day he filed your entrance folder. Do you know something about Slingshot then?"

"Only that he beat me in the Run," said Zak. "I just wondered about him, that's all. But don't worry, I'm obviously not going to find out anything else if you can't get into the file."

"I never said I couldn't get into the file," Bug murmured under his breath.

Zak shot him a look.

"I only said I didn't have clearance," Bug whispered.

"Chances are it's only been archived because it's not active any more." His eyes sparkled. "Do you want me to open it?"

"Will you get in trouble if you do?" Zak asked.

"I know how to cover my tracks," Bug said with a grin. "And I like a challenge – a brand new code to break. It'll be fun." He raised his eyebrows. "Though if I find any super-secret info, I'm going to have to log off and forget the whole thing. Deal?"

"Deal," agreed Zak. "Thanks, Bug."

Bug was about to start typing when Zak's Mob rang, playing the bouncing melody that Zak had programmed to indicate Switch was calling.

Zak put the Mob to his ear. "Yes?"

"Get up here," came Switchblade's voice. "The car's arrived and we're all waiting for you."

Zak hadn't realized the time. "Okay, give me two minutes. I just need to grab my stuff." He ended the call. "Bug – good luck with that file. You can fill me in on anything interesting later. I have to go." He ran back to his room to pick up the bag he'd packed.

Up at ground level, a car was standing in a quiet backstreet with its motor running. A car to take Zak and Wildcat and Switchblade to Heathrow Airport.

*

As the car sped along the motorway towards the airport, Zak read aloud from the file that Bug had downloaded onto his Mob.

"A recent breakthrough in CAD has allowed the design team behind TR3000 to create the first truly telepresent computer game environment with fully-realized haptic, sonic and visual input and an omnidirectional treadmill to give the player the convincing illusion of being fully integrated in the game world presented to them." Zak looked at Switch and Cat. "I know an omnidirectional treadmill is one that can go in any direction, and haptic stuff makes the virtual landscape move around you as if you're walking through it, but what's CAD, and what's telepresent?"

"CAD stands for computer-aided design," said Wildcat, not looking up from her Mob logic game. "And telepresence is technology that tricks you into thinking you're touching stuff that isn't actually there."

"So, you add all that together, and you get a computer game that feels real," said Switch. "Really real, not virtually real." He raised his eyebrows. "I'm ready to be impressed – if it's true."

"I guess we'll find that out when the game premieres in a couple of days' time," Zak said, scrolling through a long list of eye-watering techno jargon. "Here we go," he said. "The TR3000 design team has recreated in painstaking and accurate detail the world of the Mesozoic Era, incorporating the sights, smells and sounds of an environment where dinosaurs roamed free. By wearing breakthrough data-suits and cyber-helmets, the game-players will truly believe they have been transported back to the Age of the Reptiles." He grinned. "Cool!"

"Where's the premiere taking place?" asked Wildcat.

"In the Dinosaur Gallery of the Natural History Museum in Kensington," Zak read aloud. He looked up at them. "On the afternoon of the same day King Edgar is giving his big speech at the climate change conference. It says here that Prince Viktor of Montevisto will be one of the VIPs in attendance, along with the King and the rest of the Royal Family."

"Sounds like it'll be game geek heaven," said Wildcat.

Zak smiled.

Yes it did!

The pilot's voice rang through the passenger cabin of the Boeing 787. "The weather in Montevisto is fine and clear, with temperatures rising to twenty-six degrees Celsius. Our flight is on schedule and we're due to land at Montevisto International Airport at ten-forty-five local time. Please enjoy the rest of your flight."

Zak had a window seat. Beyond the oval of thick glass, the sky above the aeroplane was dazzlingly blue. Thick white clouds rolled away beneath them, breaking every now and then to reveal slow-moving mountains far below. The Pyrenees, Switch had said.

"I've been doing some extra research on MARS," Switchblade said. "I got Bug to upload some more stuff for me." His tablet computer was perched on his knees. "When they first emerged, about fifteen years ago, they produced a manifesto of their aims, and demanded that the King abdicate and declare a republic in the name of the people."

"Which people would that be?" asked Wildcat.

"The kind of people who like blowing things up and shooting innocent bystanders, from what I read in the file Control gave us," muttered Zak. "They seem to be a bunch of loonies."

Switch nodded. "Crazy and dangerous loonies," he agreed. "They never had much popular support among ordinary people. Not that they let a minor detail like that hold them back." He shook his head. "Apparently, despite the best efforts of the Montevisto Security Agencies, the name of the mastermind behind MARS has never been discovered. Various criminal bosses have been investigated, including Alfonso Gecko, a suspected gang leader who lives in Montevisto. They think he's got his dirty fingers in several of the legitimate casinos that operate there."

"Gecko?" said Zak. "That's a kind of lizard, isn't it?"

"Listen to this," said Switch. "'While no coherent plan has been discovered, internet chatter from suspected MARS operatives has been picked up containing frequent references to the Tyrant King.'"

"The Tyrant King being King Edgar?" said Wildcat.

"I guess so," said Switch, reading on. "Phrases such as, 'The death of the Tyrant King will be the death of the monarchy' recur frequently, along with, 'When the Tyrant King is blown up, the Corvetti Family will be finished.'" Switch let out a low whistle. "What do you guys make of that?"

"A bomb," said Zak uneasily. "It sounds as though they're talking about a bomb."

The pilot's voice sounded again. "We are now approaching Montevisto International Airport. Ladies and gentlemen, as we begin our descent, please turn off all electronic devices, put your seats in the upright position, secure your tray tables and fasten your seatbelts."

Zak looked out of the window again. They were much lower now, flying fast over green forests, turning in a slow arc over a sparkling blue sea. A long curved bay stretched beneath them, its shoreline crowded with buildings and marinas. And in the distance, on a promontory of white rock, Zak saw the towers and walls of the ancient castle of the Royal Family of Montevisto.

They had arrived at their destination.

CHAPTER **FOUR**

A maroon Rolls Royce Phantom was waiting for them at the airport. The three agents loaded their bags into the boot and piled into the spacious limousine. It was air conditioned and soft music was playing.

"I could get used to this," said Switch, leaning back in the plush leather seat and stretching his legs.

"I'm already there," Zak agreed.

As they drove along busy seafront streets Zak saw tourists strolling the wide pavements, and filling the outdoor tables of the fancy restaurants that overlooked the crowded marina. Behind the older buildings, modern skyscrapers glinted in the sunlight, making a strange contrast.

The car left the town and followed the road up a long hill blanketed with trees. The engine purred effortlessly on the steep rise, as though it had energy and power to spare.

A sudden worrying thought hit Zak. "What do I call them?" he asked. "The King and everyone. I can't just say, hi there, Mr King, mate, how's it going? Love your realm, by the way."

Switch grinned at him. "Call the King 'Your Majesty' first time around, then 'Sir'," he said. "The Queen is 'Your Royal Highness', then 'Ma'am'."

Sir and Ma'am. That was going to be weird.

"What about the Prince?" Zak asked.

"Same as for the Queen," Switch told him. "Except it'll be Sir instead of Ma'am."

Zak gave him a dubious look. "He's the same age I am – and I have to call him 'Your Royal Highness' and 'Sir'? You're kidding, right?"

Wildcat laughed. "You need to obey the royal protocols, Silver," she said. "That castle probably has dungeons. One wrong move and you'll find yourself chained to a wall down there."

The Roller emerged from the tunnel of trees, and

Zak's eyes widened as a breathtaking panorama opened out before them. They were high above the town now, moving rapidly along a road that clung to the brink of a cliff. The Mediterranean Sea stretched all the way to the horizon, shimmering and sparkling in the sunlight. Brightly coloured sailboats glided on the smooth blue water like exotic butterflies.

The road climbed up to the walls of the Royal Castle. Sloping rooftops and the pointed pinnacles of towers were visible above the battlements.

As they approached the gatehouse, great dark wooden doors swung open to let them in. The road ran on through ornate, formal gardens decorated with statues and trees and neat flowerbeds.

The limousine came to a gliding halt in front of an imposing entrance with wide steps and pillars. A woman, a man and a boy were waiting at the top of the steps. Men wearing red tunics appeared from nowhere to open the car doors and take the luggage from the boot.

"Welcome to the Palace of the House of Corvetti," one of the men said as Zak, Switch and Wildcat got out of the car. He had a strong French accent. "Follow me, please."

Your Majesty, then Sir. Your Royal Highness, then Ma'am, Zak repeated to himself under his breath. He had no idea why he felt so nervous. They were just *people* – except they kind of weren't.

He recognized Queen Sophia and Prince Viktor from the photographs – but the man standing with them wasn't the King. He was tall and distinguished, middle aged with a lined face and a hooked nose and dark eyes under sweeping eyebrows.

He stepped forwards to meet the three agents.

"Welcome." His voice was powerful and deep, again with an accent, but not French. German, maybe? Zak could imagine him barking orders that sent people scurrying in all directions. "I am Johannes Jorum, the King's Chancellor. King Edgar sends his apologies for not being here to greet you in person, but important matters of state have detained him."

"Not a problem, Sir," said Switchblade.

"Thank you so much for helping us," Queen Sophia said, coming forwards and shaking each of them by the hand. She was English, Zak noted from her voice. Posh English. "I hope we can make you as comfortable as possible while you are staying here."

"Anything we can do to make things easier for you, Your Royal Highness," Wildcat said.

Queen Sophia smiled. "Viktor, come and greet our guests."

The Prince walked slowly down the steps, his hands behind his back, his face solemn and stiff.

He looked at Zak. "I hope you had a good flight," he said, holding out his hand. No French accent there either.

"Yes," Zak blurted. "Thanks. It was great . . ." He left the sentence hanging. He just couldn't bring himself to call the boy "Sir". "Thanks."

"I'm told you're to be my bodyguard while I'm in London," said the Prince, unsmiling. "Does that mean your job is to throw yourself between me and a gunman's bullets? It's a rather unusual career option. How do you feel about it?"

Zak gaped. Lost for words.

"Our job, Your Royal Highness, is to make sure no gunmen get anywhere near you," said Switchblade.

The Prince lifted an eyebrow. "You seem very young for that kind of responsibility," he said.

"We're all fully trained, Sir," said Wildcat. "You really have nothing to worry about."

The Prince looked at Wildcat as though he didn't quite believe her. "Very well," he said, walking back up the steps. He paused and turned, frowning at them. "Come," he said. "Someone will show you to your rooms."

Great. He's a total weirdo, Zak thought gloomily as they followed him into the Palace. He wasn't looking forward to spending the next couple of days glued to the peculiar Prince's side.

Zak stood in the middle of his bedroom, trying to take it all in. The room was huge. The high ceiling was decorated with gold scrollwork. There was antique furniture and an enormous four-poster bed. Oil paintings on the walls depicted people with big bulging eyes wearing powdered wigs and neck ruffs.

A tall set of French windows stood open, leading to a balcony that overlooked the sea. Zak kicked his shoes off and stepped outside. The cliff was sheer, dropping away to the rocky sea line a hundred or more metres below where he was standing. "Amazing!" he said under his breath. "Totally amazing!" The briny tang of the warm sea air wafted over him. Seagulls called as they glided to and fro.

He gripped the stone balustrade, a grin widening on his face. "If they could see me now," he murmured, thinking of his old pals in Robert Wyatt House.

Only a few weeks ago he had been just another orphan in council care. Happy enough, but with no particular plans or ambitions. And now he was a member of Project 17, on a mission in a royal castle in the Med.

Wow! The way things could change.

He turned, full of bottled-up energy after the long flight. He needed to let off steam. He ran back into his room and took a flying leap onto the bed. The springs creaked and groaned as he bounced up and down, laughing.

This is unbelievable!

He trampolined on the bed until his foot caught in the rumpled covers and he fell spreadeagled on his back, gasping for breath and still laughing.

Life was great. Even the thought of having to babysit loony Prince Viktor couldn't dampen his spirits right now.

Just then, his Mob made a curious rhythmic croaking noise.

He pulled it out of his pocket. That was the call tone for Bug.

"You wouldn't believe this place!" Zak said into the phone. "It's as if it hasn't changed for hundreds of years. There are servants everywhere and all these old oil paintings on the walls. It's ridiculous. I'm not too sure about the Prince, though. I don't think we're going to be pals."

Bug cut him short. "Did you know you have an MI5 file?" he asked.

Zak sat up. "I have a what?"

"An MI5 file," Bug repeated. "I can't get into it, but it looks as though it was opened about the time you were born. You've been under MI5 surveillance your entire life."

"Why would I have an MI5 file?" Zak breathed. "Does *everyone* have an MI5 file? Is it just . . . like . . . *normal* to have an MI5 file?"

"I don't think so," came Bug's voice. "All I can tell you is that it's a Gold file – which means it has the highest security level. If I tried to get it open, it would trigger alarms all over. I only found it by chance. I thought you'd want to know."

"'Well, yes . . . thanks," Zak stammered. "Do Switch and the others have MI5 files?"

"No."

"Just me?"

"Yes."

Weird. Very weird. MI5 had been watching him since he was a baby? Why would they do that?

"I haven't had a chance to look into that other thing for you yet," said Bug. "I'm going to check it out next, if you're still interested."

"I am, thanks," mumbled Zak, assuming he was talking about Slingshot. The line went dead. Bug wasn't great on the phone. He tended not to remember to say goodbye.

Zak stared up at the ornate ceiling, baffled and confused. *An MI5 file?* He wondered if Colonel Hunter knew about it. He *must* do. He was certainly going to ask him when he got back to Fortress.

A stealthy creak caught his attention. He snapped his head around in time to see a section of the wall at the side of his bed slowly opening.

He stared, frozen for the moment, hardly able to believe his eyes.

A secret panel in the wall?

You have to be kidding me.

The panel opened wider. Something metallic and cylinder shaped came rolling across the floor. A deep, gravelly voice bellowed, "Thus perish all enemies of the revolution!"

CHAPTER **FIVE**

Bug was sitting in his default position in his little high-tech room, on the swivel chair with his feet up on the edge of the desk and the keyboard on his knees.

The door opened and suddenly Colonel Hunter was in the room.

"How's it going, Bug?" the Colonel asked. "Everything under control?"

Startled, Bug tapped the Esc key to lose the page he had been looking at. He peered up at his boss. "Everything's fine, Control," he said. "Icewater and Moonbeam are all set in Helsinki. The situation in

Tokyo is unchanged. Operation Werewolf is progressing according to plan in the Ukraine, and I'm expecting to hear from Buenos Aires within the hour."

"Excellent," said the Colonel. "And Montevisto?"

"On schedule," said Bug.

"Glad to hear it." He tapped his fingers on the back of Bug's chair. "Keep me informed," he said. Bug nodded and held his breath. The Colonel turned and headed for the door.

Bug let his breath out very slowly.

"Oh and, Bug?" said the Colonel. "Don't try to access Alpha Clearance files without my authorization. It's against the rules. You could get into trouble."

Bug heard the door click shut behind Colonel Hunter. Wincing, he strained his head around and stared uneasily at the closed door.

Busted!

He reopened the file he'd hidden. Codename Slingshot. He was about five moves away from unlocking it. He opened Search and clicked on Clear History. His finger hovered for a second, then came down on the delete key.

The page vanished.

Quicksilver was going to have to find some other way to get the information he wanted on Slingshot.

*

Zak froze only for a split second before instinct and training kicked in. He threw himself off the bed, grabbed the canister and sprinted to the window. He cannoned into the balustrade of the balcony and flung the heavy canister as hard as he could. He saw it flash in the sunlight as it curved through the shimmering air.

He ducked, counting in his head, waiting for the explosion, his heart racing.

He counted to twenty-five. Nothing. He stood up and stared over the balcony. The blue water had swallowed the metal canister. Had the seawater disabled the timer?

Then he heard slow applause behind him. Prince Viktor was standing at the French windows, dressed in scruffy jeans and T-shirt, barefoot, grinning widely and clapping his hands.

"I'm impressed," he said. "You're fast. And resourceful." He laughed, and said in the same deep, gravelly voice. "Thus perish all enemies of the revolution!"

"You idiot!" Zak shouted before he could stop himself. "What did you do that for?"

The smile fell from Prince Viktor's face. His blue eyes gleamed. "No one speaks to me like that," he spat. "I could have you beheaded for your insolence."

Zak stared at the Prince. He knew he shouldn't have lost his temper. All the same . . .

"Beheaded?" he gasped. "Are you mental?"

Prince Viktor grinned again. He strode across the balcony and stared down into the sea. "It was a tin of asparagus tips with the label torn off, in case you were wondering," he said, resting one elbow on the balustrade and looking at Zak. "If I'm going to trust you to protect me, I think I'm entitled to test your abilities," he continued. "Did you really think it was a bomb?"

"I don't know what I thought," Zak replied. "I didn't have time to think anything at all." He frowned. "I've been told I should call you *Sir*."

The Prince shrugged. "Viktor will do," he said. "Were you scared? Did you think you were going to be blown to pieces?"

Not for the first time, Zak didn't know how to respond. "You're a bit weird, do you know that?" he said at last.

"In my defence, I do," said Viktor amiably. "You'd be weird too if you'd had my upbringing. I was told you're interested in dinosaurs. Which is your favourite?"

Zak did his best to follow this conversational swerve. "I like the big herbivores like Apatosaurus," he said. "But the raptors are cool too."

Viktor nodded. "I like the Spinosaurus. I'm a big

fan of the carnivores. Did you see the movie where a Spinosaurus fought a T-rex?"

Zak nodded. "It was fine, except that it could never have happened – they lived, like, millions of years apart."

Viktor's eyes gleamed in pleasure. "Absolutely correct," he said. "I think we're going to get on. Come with me."

Viktor led Zak through the panel. There was a short stone tunnel and then another door into a room of a similar size to Zak's.

"I call this my Mesozoic Madhouse," Viktor said, with a note of pride in his voice. "What do you think?"

This was obviously the Prince's bedroom, but the walls were covered in posters of dinosaurs, and an entire army of dinosaurs was assembled in a series of glass display cabinets and on long tables. Some were just the kind of plastic toys you could find in shops, but others were intricately assembled resin skeletons or replicas that stood two or more metres tall.

Zak didn't like to say what he really thought – that Prince Viktor must be out of his mind to want to sleep in a room full of all this stuff.

"Amazing," he murmured. "Totally amazing!"

"Isn't it, though?" said the Prince, grinning.

On a wide screen on the wall opposite his bed, a

film was playing silently. Zak recognized scenes from *Jurassic Park* and *Godzilla* and *The Lost World* and *King Kong*, all edited together on a continuous loop.

"Have you seen the teaser for TR3000?" Viktor asked, beckoning Zak over to the projector set up in the middle of the room. "It's awesome!" He pressed some buttons and the movie-clip show changed to a video of a small group of people dressed in silvery jumpsuits and wearing helmets with deep visors.

A husky, dramatic voice introduced the TR3000, while the people in the strange suits moved about, grabbing at things that weren't there, walking on treadmills, ducking to avoid non-existent obstacles, and sometimes standing and staring up at something huge that only they could see.

Then there were interviews with the people. They all looked amazed and stunned, talking breathlessly about how realistic the gaming experience had been.

Viktor's eyes shone. "They're holding back shots of the actual game till the premiere," he said. "I've been waiting for this for three months, ever since I heard about it," he said. "And in a couple of days I'm going to be in the Natural History Museum in London, playing the first ever full game."

"It looks great," Zak admitted.

"Do you like computer games?" Viktor asked.

Zak nodded.

"Excellent – then we'll play one! It won't be as good as TR3000, but we'll make do. If you beat me, I'll make you a Noble Knight of Montevisto. If you lose, you sleep in the Torture Chamber. Strapped to the rack. Okay?"

Zak laughed. "Okay!" He was getting used to the Prince's sense of humour.

In the end, Zak didn't get much time to play games with the Prince. A few minutes in, his Mob rang. Chancellor Jorum was ready to give the Project 17 team their briefing.

Zak and Wildcat and Switchblade were brought to a long room dominated by a massive polished oak table. The Chancellor showed them maps and plans of the castle and the route to the airport that the Royal Family would take the following day. "For security purposes, the Prince does not fly with the King and Queen," he explained. "Prince Viktor will travel in advance of the rest of the Royal Family, and his security will be in your hands throughout the trip. Do you understand?"

"We understand perfectly, Sir," said Switchblade. "Do you have a timetable for the visit?"

"I do," said the Chancellor, handing out thick wedges of stapled documents. Zak scanned a long list of the minute-by-minute movements that were planned for the Prince – from the exact time he would be picked up outside the Palace for the journey to Montevisto International Airport, all the way to the precise moment he would be checking into the Berwick Hotel in the heart of London, and beyond. There were ten pages of it.

Then there were more briefing papers on MARS and another big chunk of background information and protocols.

"I cannot stress enough the importance of your mission," the Chancellor said, looking from face to face with his fierce dark eyes. "Nothing must happen to the Prince, do you understand?" he paused. "I am told by the very highest authorities in your country that I can rely on you, despite your youth."

"You can, Sir," said Wildcat. "The Prince will be safe with us."

Jorum nodded curtly. "So be it," he said. "You will be expected to attend the banquet this evening. I trust you have brought formal dress?"

"We have," Switchblade said.

We have? thought Zak. *Since when?*

"Excellent." The Chancellor stood up. "You may now

go about your business."

He swept out of the room.

"Formal dress?" asked Zak. "What formal dress?"

"Control had me pack a penguin suit for you," Switch said with a smile. "Don't worry – you'll look great in a tuxedo."

Zak wasn't sure about that.

Zak stared at himself in the full-length mirror.

"You look like an idiot," he told his reflection. "A total and utter idiot."

He was dressed in a black dinner jacket and trousers, and a stiff white shirt that was buttoned up tightly around his neck. But the worst thing was the black bowtie. It made him look as though he was being strangled by a bat!

"Not at all," said Wildcat, standing behind him and tweaking the bowtie to straighten it up. "You know what? You look like James Bond Junior."

Zak raised an eyebrow. "The name's Silver," he drawled into the mirror. "*Quick* . . . Silver."

Wildcat laughed and slapped her hands down on his shoulders. "You'll do," she said. He turned around. Wildcat didn't look so bad herself. She was wearing a simple black dress and she'd even tamed her hair so it didn't look quite so much as if she'd just put her tongue into an electric socket.

The door opened. Switch came in. He looked a bit bizarre but also rather impressive in his formal clothes.

"Everyone ready?" he said. "Come on then, now we get to meet the King."

The banquet was a huge, glamorous affair. Zak guessed there must be fifty or more guests at the immense table: dignitaries and celebrities and bigwigs from all over the world. He thought he heard French and German and Italian for sure, and possibly even some Russian and Japanese. The three Project 17 agents were sitting at the far end of the table from the royals. Zak had been wondering what he'd say to the King, but in the event, he'd have needed a megaphone to say anything at all.

As the lengthy meal progressed, Zak noticed that there was one unoccupied chair up the far end. At one point he saw the King gesture towards it in an annoyed manner. The Queen shook her head and Chancellor Jorum called a servant over, then sent him away. The servant came back a few minutes later and whatever he said clearly irritated the King even more.

A while later, Viktor slipped out of his seat and came to see how the three of them were doing.

"My father is in one of his moods," the Prince told them quietly. "He ordered my cousin Rafe to attend, but he hasn't turned up."

That explained the empty chair.

"He'll probably stroll in when everyone's finished," Viktor added. "If he bothers at all." Zak thought he detected a hint of envy in his voice, as though the Prince wished he could come and go as he pleased.

The banquet lasted several hours, but when it eventually broke up, Zak, Switch and Wildcat headed to their rooms for the night. They said goodnight and Zak walked along the corridor to his own room. He heard running feet behind him. It was Viktor.

"What did you think of that?" he asked Zak.

"Interesting," Zak said guardedly.

"You think?" Viktor said in surprise. "I hate functions where Father and Mother have to suck up to a lot of foreign diplomats and businessmen and VIPs." He shook his head. "It wouldn't be so bad if they left me out of it, but I have to show my face and be polite. The Crown Prince! That's me, whether I like it or not. As if I want to be king. I'd rather be a racing driver. Formula One, you know? But everyone says it's too dangerous. It drives me crazy." He made another of his conversational jumps. "Want to play some more games? I've got dozens – we could make a night of it."

"I can't," Zak said reluctantly. "I need to be up early." He gave a rueful half-smile. "I'm not going to be in any condition to leap in front of bullets if I've been up half the night."

"Shame," said Viktor. "Maybe tomorrow morning?" The sound of approaching feet made them both turn around.

Zak recognized Prince Rafe immediately. The Prince was wearing a brown leather jacket and a white silk scarf. His hair was tousled as though he'd been out in a high wind.

"Where have you been?" cried Viktor. "Do you know how much trouble you're in with my parents?"

"They will get over it," said Rafe, and Zak noticed that he spoke with a strong French accent. "It would have been *si ennuyeux* – so boring! I have better things to do than sit around listening to a bunch of idiots." His grin widened. "And who is your little friend?" he asked, looking Zak up and down. "A new playmate?"

"He's my bodyguard for the London trip," said Viktor. "He's okay."

Rafe nodded briefly at Zak, then seemed to dismiss him as he addressed the Prince. "I've picked up the new car, Viktor. *Elle est belle!* A beauty – a real charmer! I've just driven her back here from the dealer's."

Zak saw Viktor's eyes light up with excitement. "What did you go for in the end?"

"A Peugeot 207, S2000," said Prince Rafe. "Rear spoilers. Tubular roll cage. Hydraulic handbrake. Sequential six-speed gearbox. Four-wheel drive and three automatic-locking differentials."

"Can I see it?" asked Viktor.

"We can do better than that, little cousin," said Rafe. "Meet me at the Ellipse in half an hour – I'll take you for a night-time drive. *À bientôt!*" And with that, Prince Rafe strode away down the corridor and disappeared.

Zak looked uneasily at Prince Viktor. "You're not really going with him, are you?" he asked.

"Of course I am," said Viktor.

"You can't do that," Zak insisted. "I'm supposed to . . . you know . . . make sure you're okay. You can't just go for a drive in the middle of the night. My boss would go crazy."

Viktor smiled. "Then I suggest you don't tell him," he said. "Goodnight, my friend. Sweet dreams."

"But . . ."

Viktor opened the door to his room, walked in and closed it behind him. Zak stood in the hallway, feeling rather stupid.

Being on Prince Viktor's protection detail wasn't going to be quite as easy as he'd hoped.

CHAPTER **SIX**

Zak sat on the edge of his bed, dressed now in T-shirt and jeans. He was staring through the open French windows at a patch of velvet-black sky sprinkled with bright stars. He'd never seen so many stars in his life. Unfortunately he had other things on his mind right now.

He had his Mob in his hand and he was trying to decide what to do about the Prince. Call Colonel Hunter?

Help! Viktor's being a pain and I don't know what to do about it.

Oh, poor you. Come and tell Control all about it.

No way. That wasn't an option. He might as well pack

up and go home.

Go and see Switch or Cat? Tell them that the Prince was planning a midnight escapade with his cousin?

He could already hear Switchblade's voice in his head. *Okay, Silver, you go to bed, we'll deal with it for you.*

Don't worry your little head about it.

No! No! No!

Zak slid the Mob into his pocket and crossed to the hidden panel. He ran his hands over the wall, feeling for a trigger or switch. A small section of the wainscoting was loose. He twisted it aside and the panel swung open. He took a deep breath as he stepped into the short tunnel.

"Don't take no for an answer," he murmured under his breath. "Tell him he can't go out. Definitely. No way." He pushed at the second panel. It didn't move. He felt around in the half-dark, but there was no obvious way to unlock it.

He knocked. A few moments passed before the panel swung open. Viktor peered at Zak from under the peak of a baseball cap. He was wearing jeans and a casual jacket.

"Shouldn't you be in bed?" Viktor asked, opening the panel wider to let Zak through. "I thought you needed a good night's sleep."

"You can't go for a drive." Zak tried his best to phrase this in the way Colonel Hunter would have done. As if it was an order.

"I think you'll find I can," Viktor replied with an unconcerned smile. "Don't worry. Rafe is a very good driver."

Zak frowned. "That's not the point. I'm meant to keep tabs on you."

"Relax," said Viktor. "Your job doesn't really start until we get to London. Listen, I'll be back in an hour or so and no one will ever know I was gone."

Zak took a sharp breath. "If you go, I'll have to call my boss," he said.

Viktor shrugged. "Please yourself," he said, walking towards the door. "I'm going." He gave Zak a hard look. "But if my father hears I've been out with Rafe he'll be angry. He'll punish me for sure. I expect he'll cancel my trip to London." His eyes narrowed. "Is that what you want?"

Zak stared at him. If he told on Viktor and the Prince's trip to London was cancelled, the Project 17 mission would be over before it began. He definitely didn't want that to happen. This was his first mission – he wanted to see it through, not wreck it.

"I can't talk you out of it?" he asked.

Viktor shook his head.

Zak thought fast. He didn't want to cause trouble for the Prince. But he couldn't just let him wander off like that. Control would go ballistic.

"I'm coming with you," he said at last.

A grin spread across Viktor's face. "Excellent," he said. "This is going to be awesome!"

Viktor led Zak through deserted corridors and down several flights of stairs. There was hardly anyone about at this time of night, but the Prince was cautious – always making sure the coast was clear before he moved on. Almost the way a Project 17 agent would do, Zak thought.

Zak patted the pocket with his Mob in it. If anything went wrong, he could always call Switch or Cat for back up.

All they were doing was going for a night-time drive. What could possibly go wrong?

Viktor led Zak out under a curved stone portico. Prince Rafe was leaning against the front of a sleek two-door rally car. It was gleaming white, with tinted windows and a high rear wing.

"I see you have brought your little friend with you," said Rafe. "We will all ride together, yes?"

Viktor ran his hands over the smooth contours of the car. "She's beautiful," he said. "What can she do?"

"Get in and I will show you," said Rafe.

Zak had to squeeze into the back. The car smelled new and expensive. Rafe and Viktor climbed in. Rafe looked at Zak over his shoulder.

"Are you ready for some fun, *mon ami*?" he asked.

"You bet," Zak replied, thinking the opposite.

"Buckle up, *mes enfants*!" Rafe turned the key in the ignition. "The night is young!" The engine growled, like a waking tiger. The white beams of the headlights flooded the gravel pathway. The car vibrated, roaring now – wide awake and eager to go. Zak could feel the power building as the engine revved. He found the seatbelt and strapped himself in tightly.

Then they were away into the night, picking up speed at an alarming rate. Zak clung on grimly as Rafe steered around a sharp bend in the path and shot between tall hedges.

In any other circumstances, Zak would have loved this – but as they sped along, all he could think was: *What if Rafe drives us into a tree? How am I going to explain this to Control?*

The car skidded to a halt at a set of wrought-iron gates in a long wall. Viktor jumped out and opened the gates.

"Are we going far?" Zak asked Rafe.

"This is a small country, *mon ami*," Rafe replied with a grin. "We cannot go so very far. Do not fear, I am – as they say – the tip-top driver." He laughed. "*Je suis le meilleur*! The very best!"

Viktor climbed back in and the car shot through the gateway and onto the open road.

What alarmed Zak most as they raced along was the fact that there were no street lights. Nothing at all, in fact, except for the wide rake of the headlight beams, lighting up the road directly ahead of them. It was as if they were plunging headlong down a black grass-edged tunnel that swerved from side to side with only a moment's warning. Zak was amazed Rafe didn't drive them off the road in those first few frantic minutes.

"Is this as fast as she goes?" asked Viktor as they raced along a narrow stretch of road lined with trees.

"You wish for faster?" asked Rafe.

No, thought Zak, envisaging the morning headlines, *I really don't.*

Heir to the throne of Montevisto found dead in the mangled wreckage of a car. Also killed in the accident were Prince Rafe and some idiot English kid who nobody cares about.

"Put your foot down, Rafe," urged Viktor. "Show us what she can do!"

"Hold onto your hats, *mes amis*!" shouted Rafe. "Let's put *la belle* through her paces!"

The car sped up, jerking Zak back into his seat. The trees rushed by and suddenly they were on a road that twisted and turned as it wound its way across the hills.

The road plunged between two high shoulders of rock and burst into the open again, curving as it hugged a cliff edge. Only a few metres away, the world came to an abrupt end above the sea. One wrong move and . . .

Zak decided not to think about it now.

There'd be plenty of time for that as they plummeted to their certain deaths.

Still, it wasn't all bad. At least the two *Princes* were having a great time. Viktor was constantly asking Rafe to go faster and faster, and Rafe went for it, whooping and hollering as they took hairpin bends at crazy speeds and bounced over sudden humpbacks, all four wheels off the road at once.

One thing was for sure: Rafe could drive.

As Rafe negotiated one perilous bend after another, Zak began to calm down. His heart rate returned to normal and he unclenched his fists. Rafe knew what he was doing. They'd be fine.

And it was kind of fun.

Zak smiled to himself. In fact, it was a whole lot of fun once you stopped worrying and just let yourself go with the flow.

"So, who are you dating now?" Viktor asked his cousin as they hurtled down a long, straight hill. "Is it still Sasha the supermodel, or are you bored with her already?"

"No, no, Sasha is history, long time now," said Rafe, laughing. "A very dull woman indeed. Since her, I have been out with Coco and Evangelina and Laetitia. All very nice young women, very attractive, very intelligent. Laetitia has a new song in the charts right now." He winked at Zak. "A woman should have brains and charm and talent as well as beauty, would you not say, *mon ami*?"

"Oh, absolutely," said Zak, just about managing to keep a straight face. "They need all four to have a chance with me."

"Laetitia is my good-luck charm," Rafe said as they skidded around a tight bend and shot along another long straight stretch of road. "When I go with her to the casinos, I always win big. Roulette, blackjack, baccarat. She is – what do you say in English? – my hare's paw!"

"Rabbit's foot," said Zak.

"You're winning again now?" asked Viktor. "The losing streak is over?"

"What losing streak, little cousin?" said Rafe, laughing. "There is no losing streak. There never was a losing streak."

Zak thought he saw Viktor give his cousin an uncertain look, but he said no more about it.

Up to now on their madcap ride through the night, they had not encountered a single other vehicle. Zak was beginning to think that the whole of Montevisto went to bed early. Except that every so often the road would run along a high ridge and he'd see the coloured lights of the town twinkling below them. Montevisto definitely had a nightlife – and quite a lively one from what Rafe had been saying, teeming with supermodels and pop stars and casinos.

The first Zak knew of the car that came speeding up behind them was a dazzle of white lights in the rear-view mirror.

Viktor twisted around. "I think we're being followed," he said.

Zak turned as well. He could see nothing of the upcoming car behind the glare of the headlights. Just a vague black blur. But it was moving fast, eating up the distance between them, closing in.

"They must be in a hurry," Viktor remarked, squinting in the bright glare. "Move over, Rafe. Let them pass. Maybe there's some kind of emergency."

Rafe guided the car to the side of the road, but he didn't slow down. The other car gradually crept up alongside them. It was black and Zak could see two occupants – both men, visible only as silhouettes.

For a few moments the two cars sped along side by side. Zak saw Rafe flick a glance towards the driver. Then the Peugeot made a sudden leap forwards, accelerating fast, pinning Zak back into his seat.

The black car fell behind.

"That's it! A race!" cried Viktor. "Come on, Rafe! You can beat them!"

Prince Rafe was silent now, his knuckles white as he gripped the steering wheel, his body tense and hunched.

For a few seconds, it seemed that they would leave the other car standing, but slowly it began to catch up again.

Zak heard Rafe muttering under his breath, and there was urgency and alarm in his voice now. "*Ils ne seront pas m'attraper!*"

What did it mean? Zak mouthed the words to himself so as to fix them in his mind. Rafe had spat the sentence very fiercely, and he seemed so different from the lighthearted person he'd been only a few moments earlier, that Zak felt sure it must have significance. Something was definitely wrong. Rafe's whole attitude had changed. Even Viktor had gone quiet.

The black car pulled alongside the Peugeot and swerved suddenly towards them.

With a stifled cry, Rafe wrenched at the steering wheel as the two cars came into contact. There was a scream of metal as the black car rammed them off the road. Zak threw his arms up to cover his face as he was thrown around inside the car like a rag doll and the world turned over and over around him.

CHAPTER **SEVEN**

Zak hung upside down in his seat in absolute darkness and silence. For a few moments he was so dazed that he had no idea where he was. Then he heard groans and his mind snapped back into action.

The dazzle of headlights behind them. The black car cruising alongside. The horrible screech as they had been rammed off the road. The disorienting spinning, and the sickening lurch as they came to a final halt.

"Is everyone okay?" he gasped, feeling for the buckle of his seatbelt.

He heard Rafe murmur something in French.

Zak stretched one hand up to the inverted roof of the car as he freed himself. Then he dropped down in a tangle of arms and legs. There was some pain, especially across his chest and waist where the seat belt had bitten into him.

He struggled to get upright in the pitch-blackness. He felt in his pocket for the pencil torch, hoping it hadn't been broken in the crash. His fingers closed around it and he pulled it out, flicking the switch. A bright beam raked through the upturned car.

Rafe and Viktor were hanging upside down as Zak had been – but they were both conscious.

"Can you get the doors open?" Zak said.

Rafe released his seatbelt, falling and manoeuvering himself into a crouching position. There was blood on his forehead and his eyes looked wild in the torchlight. He wrestled for a few moments with the door, but it didn't give. Zak aimed his torch out of the side window. They seemed to have landed in heavy undergrowth. He could see broken branches and leaves pressing against the glass. A soft landing – of sorts. It had probably saved their lives.

Rafe helped Viktor, supporting him while the young Prince undid his seatbelt and came slithering down. Viktor looked bewildered and frightened, but Zak was relieved to see that there was nothing to suggest serious injury. Leafy branches blocked the passenger window too and the door would not move, not even when Rafe thrust his hands against it and Viktor kicked with both feet.

Suddenly Zak had a horrible thought.

"Have you switched the ignition off?" he asked.

"Why? What does it matter?" gasped Rafe.

"If the electrics are still on and petrol is leaking, the whole car could go up in flames!" Zak said. "Check it! Now!"

Rafe groped at the steering column. "It is off," he said.

"Good." Zak took out his Mob. "Even if we could kick out the windows, we'll never get through those branches. I'm going to call for help." He pressed the screen. He touched the contacts icon and scrolled to Switchblade's name.

Was this an appropriate moment to use the ultimate emergency codeword: Winter? Only when lives were in imminent danger, Control had said. The way things were, their lives weren't in danger. Winter could wait.

All the same, Zak thought, this was gong to be a very awkward conversation.

*

Zak stood on the road in the intermeshing cross-beams of glaring headlights. He felt like a rabbit about to be run down from several directions at once. There were five cars and an ambulance on site. The ambulance doors were open. Victor was sitting in the back with a blanket around his shoulders, drinking something from a plastic cup while paramedics buzzed around him.

Two of the vehicles were police cars, and the other three had come from the Palace. Agents of royal security had climbed down from the road and used brute forced to turn the Peugeot onto its wheels. The branches of the smashed bushes had been ripped away and the three passengers released. The two Princes had been quickly bundled up the slope by men who didn't even seem to notice Zak standing there. He had climbed the steep hill on his own, and the first face he'd seen at the top had been Switchblade's.

Before Zak could open his mouth to explain, Switch had put up his hand. "Later," he'd said. "Are you okay?"

Zak had nodded and Switch had gone to check on the Princes.

Rafe was having an argument in French with a couple of the security men. He seemed angry and disturbed, and although Zak understood virtually nothing of what was being said, he got the impression that Prince

Rafe was trying hard to dismiss the whole event as an unfortunate accident.

Zak was not so sure.

He walked over to Viktor and sat beside him. The paramedics had finished whatever they had been doing and the young Prince was drinking from a cup and looking very sorry for himself.

"Are you going to say, 'I told you so'?" Viktor asked Zak.

"I wasn't," Zak replied. "But I can if you like."

Viktor sighed heavily. "My father isn't going to let me go to London now, that's for sure," he said.

"Your cousin is doing a lot of shouting," Zak said, looking over to where Rafe was still arguing with the security men from the Palace.

"He's telling them it was nothing," Viktor replied. "The other car came too close and – boom – we went off the road." He gave a weak smile. "He's explaining to them that the Peugeot 207 has an impact-tested body-shell and a tubular roll cage. Basically, he's saying that you could have rolled us down the side of Mont Blanc and we'd have come out of it unscathed."

"Do you think it was just an accident?" Zak asked, giving Viktor a sideways look.

The Prince frowned. "I think it was a race that went wrong," he said. "I don't think they meant to do us any harm – they just wanted to win. The driver meant to nudge us a little – and he miscalculated."

"So, you don't think—" Zak was interrupted by more Palace security. They spoke rapidly to Viktor in French. He made a brief reply then got up and followed them to one of the cars. He glanced back at Zak. "My father wants to speak to Rafe and I," he said. "Wish us luck!"

Zak watched as the two Princes were bundled into one of the cars. It sped away with a shriek of rubber.

Zak stared at his shoes. This was such a mess. His first real test on his first real mission, and he'd blown it.

A shadow fell over him. He looked up. It was Switchblade.

"We're going back," he said gruffly. "I've spoken to Control. He wants to know how this happened. Wildcat is waiting for us with an open video link."

The three agents of Project 17 were gathered in Wildcat's room. They were not happy bunnies.

Wildcat's laptop was set up on a small side table. Zak, Cat and Switch were sitting facing it. Colonel Hunter's head and shoulders filled the screen. He had the look of someone dragged out of bed at one o'clock in the morning. His face was grim.

"I have just come off the phone with King Edgar," he growled. "The two Princes will not now be travelling to London. Your mission in Montevisto is terminated. You will spend the night at the Palace then take the first available flight back to London in the morning." There was a pause. Zak almost wished he'd been killed in the crash – anything would be better than this. *Anything.*

"I don't need to tell you how badly this reflects on Project 17," Colonel Hunter continued. "I assured the King you three were up to the job of protecting Prince Viktor, and . . ."

"Don't blame Switchblade and Wildcat," said Zak. "They didn't know about it. They thought the Prince was safe in bed. It was my fault."

"When I send agents on a mission, they go as a team," said the Colonel. "You celebrate success as a team; you deal with failure as a team. Switchblade and Wildcat bear the same responsibility as you, Quicksilver." The Colonel's eyes flickered and some of the anger seemed to drain from his face. "I shouldn't have sent you into the field only half-trained," he said. "I overestimated you." He reached towards the screen. "We'll discuss this at greater length when you get back to Fortress."

"Am I being thrown out?" gasped Zak. He had to know. If this was the end of him and Project 17, he'd rather be told now.

"I haven't had time to make that decision yet," said the Colonel, and the next moment he was gone and the angular P17 logo filled the screen.

Cat closed the laptop. "Well," she said. "That's that."

Switch leaned back in his chair, blowing his cheeks out, staring at the ceiling.

Zak got up, ashamed and full of useless rage. "Come on," he shouted. "Tell me what an idiot I was. I know you're both dying to say it."

"What would be the point?" asked Switch. "Control was right – we're all to blame. Cat and I were here to keep an eye on you, and we failed."

"I thought I could handle it," said Zak, his anger deflating. "I didn't want to come running to you two."

"Rookie mistake," Wildcat said mildly. "You should never be afraid to ask for help if you think you're out of your depth."

"Everything would have been fine if not for that other car," said Zak. "And I'm telling you, that was no accident. Never!"

Switch shook his head. "Both Prince Rafe and Prince Viktor say it was – they said it was a race that went wrong."

Zak looked at them. "Do either of you speak any French?" he asked.

"*Un peu,*" replied Wildcat, holding up her hand, finger and thumb a fraction apart. "School French."

Zak frowned, dredging his memory. "Rafe said something when he saw who was in the car," he said. "It sounded like . . . *ill ner seron pa mat-rapper.*" He looked at Wildcat. "Does that sound as if it means anything?"

Wildcat narrowed her eyes, thinking. "*Ils ne seront pas m'attraper?*" she said.

"Yes! That was it," said Zak. "What does it mean?"

"It means 'they will not catch me'," said Wildcat, glancing at Switchblade.

"He could have meant, they won't catch up with the car," said Switch.

"No!" said Zak. "The other car was already up alongside us when he said it. Besides, wouldn't he have said 'they won't catch *us*'?"

"He's right," said Wildcat. "Rafe was talking about himself."

"He knew the people in the car, and he was scared of them," insisted Zak. "Everything changed when that car appeared. Up until then he'd been laughing and joking and everything had been fine." He looked from Switchblade to Wildcat. "You have to believe me," he said fiercely. "That wasn't an accident."

"You should have told Control," said Switch.

"Like I was given time to explain things!" exclaimed Zak.

"The Princes have already insisted it was an accident," Cat reminded them. She gave Zak a sympathetic look. "Your credibility is going to be pretty low right now," she said. "If Rafe and Viktor stick to their story, I don't think anyone's going to believe you."

"But *you* do, don't you?" Zak asked, looking anxiously from one to the other.

"We do," said Switch. "But there's not much useful we can do right now." He gave Wildcat a questioning look.

She frowned, shrugging. "If we were staying, I'd suggest we keep an eye on Rafe," she said. "But the way it is, that's not going to be an option."

Zak looked at them gloomily. At least they still had *some* faith in him – despite everything.

"When we get back to Fortress, I think you should tell Control," said Switch. "Give him a full report on everything that happened. He'll know what to do." He stood up, stretching. "We should get to bed. Cat? Can you check on the early flights out of Montevisto International Airport? I'd like us to be gone as soon as possible tomorrow."

*

Zak lay in bed. Wide awake. Horribly awake. Miserably awake.

Every now and then he would check his Mob to see just how slowly the minutes were crawling past.

He had made such a fool of himself. He'd let everyone down. No wonder Switchblade and Wildcat weren't entirely convinced that the men in the other car had targeted Rafe on purpose. Stupid, stupid, stupid!

He kept replaying the confrontation with Viktor in his mind, rewriting it so that he managed to convince the Prince not to go out with his cousin.

It was amazing how persuasive he could be now that it was too late to matter. In a few hours, he'd be back in London – back at Fortress. Possibly for the last time.

He remembered the faces of Paul and Kath, the residential social workers at Robert Wyatt House – their expressions of pride and astonishment when Colonel Hunter had come to pick him up and take him away. They'd been told that Zak had been chosen to take part in an important National Fast-Track Scholarship Course. They were given all the necessary documents of guardianship, signed by all the right people. No mention of Project 17 and the British Secret Services, of course, but everyone at Robert Wyatt House had been impressed.

And now? If Colonel Hunter decided to cut him loose, what would happen to him? Would he be sent back to the children's home in disgrace? How humiliating would that be?

And how would he explain it to Dodge? That would almost be the worst thing of all. Dodge would be sympathetic, but he'd be so disappointed in him.

Zak threw his arms over his face, trying to blot the future out.

A weight came thumping down on the bed beside him. Something hard and narrow was pressed to his throat. "Thus die all enemies of the revolution!" snarled a gravelly voice.

"Get off me!" Zak snapped irritably, pushing the hand away. He was not in the mood for Viktor's stupid jokes.

The Prince leaned over and switched on the bedside light.

"Get out," Zak spat. "I'm sick of you and your tricks." He pulled himself up onto his elbows, glaring at the Prince. "Thanks to you my whole life is about to go down the tubes. Thanks to you, I'm . . ." He choked, too angry to carry on.

The Prince looked at him, his head tilted to one side, a comb in one hand – a comb that he had been using as a fake knife.

"You should relax," he said with a sudden grin. "You take things too seriously."

Zak stared at him, almost lost for words. "You really are mental," he said. "There's no way you're going to London now."

"That's. Where. You're. Wrong," said the Prince, tapping his comb on Zak's forehead in time with the words. His grin widened until Zak got the feeling it might actually meet around the back of his head. "I've just come back from an interview with my father, and everything's fine."

"What?" Zak sat up, amazed. "How?"

"Well, Father and Mother were very angry at first," Viktor explained. "And Father ranted and raved for a while, as he does, and Mother said how we'd let her down. But then the Chancellor stepped in, and he said it had all been just a silly bit of youthful high jinks and that no real harm had been done, and that we'd both learned a worthwhile lesson." Viktor shook his head. "At first, Father argued, but the Chancellor insisted that we'd already been punished enough in the crash." Viktor sounded surprised. "He even spoke up for Rafe, and I thought he hated him. But he insisted that the trip to London should go ahead with all four of us. He won Mother over – and in the end they managed to convince my father too." Viktor spread his arms. "So everything is fine."

"For you, maybe," said Zak. "But I'm still going to . . ." He was interrupted by the melodic ring of his Mob. Switchblade's tune. He put it to his ear.

"I'm guessing you weren't asleep," came Switch's voice.

"Chance would be a fine thing," said Zak.

"I've just heard from Control," Switch said. "The King called him again. Apparently everything's been smoothed over. The Princes are still going to London, and we're still on security detail."

"Really?" Zak could hardly believe his ears.

"Don't get too excited," added Switch. "We're still in for a massive telling-off when we get back, but for now, everything's still on track." Switch chuckled. "Now you can get some sleep," he said, ending the call.

Zak put his Mob down.

"Good news, I hope?" said Viktor.

Zak nodded. "We're not being sent home after all," he said.

"Excellent!" said the Prince, bouncing off the bed. "I'll see you in the morning." He vanished through the wall panel.

Zak let out a long, slow breath.

Maybe his new life wasn't quite so doomed after all.

CHAPTER **EIGHT**

The trilling of the Mob alarm woke Zak. He groped to shut it off. He felt as if he'd had his head down for about fifteen seconds. A pale light was filtering through the curtains.

He looked at the time on his Mob. 05:45.

He lay staring at the shadowy ceiling for a few moments, feeling drowsiness creeping up over him again.

"Get up!" he ordered himself. "Get up and get dressed right now."

He'd messed up enough for the time being – he didn't

want Switch or Cat having to come and find him in the middle of the morning.

He went into the bathroom and splashed cool water on his face.

"What you need is a run," he told his reflection.

He was about to leave the bathroom when he paused and looked into the mirror again. "New day, new start, okay?" he said.

His reflection nodded.

He opened the curtains and the silvery light of the early morning flooded the room. The sun was throwing splinters of dazzling light over the water. He breathed deeply. The air smelled good.

New day. New start.

He remembered that Switch had been planning an early morning jog. He didn't want to see Switchblade. He wanted to be alone for a while. Alone in the zone.

He pulled on some clothes and shoes and stepped into the corridor. He gazed at the long carpeted expanse with its oil paintings and half-tables against the walls, and its ornate doorways and carved plaster ceiling.

Then he turned and began to jog along the corridor, looking for a way out. He found some French windows that opened on a set of half-moon stone steps which led to gravel pathways through flowerbeds lined with neatly trimmed hedges. He closed the glass doors behind him and pattered down the steps, his lungs filling with fresh morning air, the sky pale and clear above him.

He began to run. Not too fast to begin with. Warming up his muscles, shaking off the last scraps of sleep.

He turned a corner. A long straight path lay ahead of him, bordered with tall square-cut hedges. He focused on the middle distance, arms pumping at his sides, his strides lengthening, his breath coming and going, smooth as silk.

Zak was in the zone almost before he knew it, taking curves in the pathway without losing speed, racing through the expansive gardens, gulping in the sweet early morning air. And as he ran, all the problems and the troubles and the mistakes of the previous day were left behind.

This was what he had been born for. This was how life should be. The freedom. The incredible buzz.

Zak lost all track of time as he ran, but when he came barrelling around a bend to find the morning sun shining in his face, he knew it was time to get back. He cruised alongside the palace, looking for a way back in. He couldn't find the curved steps that led to the French windows. He didn't think he was even outside the same wing.

He came to the Ellipse – the exit where Rafe had been waiting with the car last night. He could have saved everyone a lot of trouble if he'd snatched the keys from the reckless Prince and thrown them into the sea.

Luckily, the doors were unlocked. Entering, Zak heard voices and the sounds of movement. Clearly things were beginning to stir in the Palace. He padded soft-footed along a corridor, barely out of breath after his long workout.

He passed a semi-open door. A voice drifted out. He paused. It was Chancellor Jorum, and he sounded agitated.

"I agree, Sir," he was saying. "Prince Rafe's lifestyle is beyond the pale. Quite deplorable. I have no argument with that, Sir. None at all."

"And yet you still insist I allow him to go to London?" Zak recognized the King's voice. Maybe he was not quite as convinced about letting the two Princes go to London as Viktor had hoped. "I have just been shown proof that the boy has debts with several different casinos – debts running into many thousands of Euros. Had I known this a few hours ago, I would never have been persuaded to overlook his stupidity last night."

Zak's ears pricked up. Viktor had said something in the car about a losing streak, but Rafe had brushed it aside. Now perhaps Zak had the chance to learn more. He crept to the side of the door and listened intently.

"Prince Rafe must learn that his actions have consequences," stormed the King. "His lifestyle disgraces us all."

"You are entirely correct, Sir,'" said the Chancellor. "And I agree that something must be done to curb the Prince's excesses."

"What do you recommend?" snapped the King. "Should I pay his debts again, in return for another speech full of empty remorse and shallow promises of reform?"

"No, Sir," said the Chancellor. "The Prince must pay his own debts this time, as you told him would be the case last year. But I have a plan, Sir, if you will hear me out."

"Go on." The King's voice was a little calmer, although Zak had an inkling now of why that terrorist organization called him the "Tyrant King". He certainly did have a ferocious temper.

"I will broker a deal with those to whom he owes money," Jorum explained. "I will have the Prince banned from every casino in Montevisto, and I will work out a way for him to pay back his debts in instalments."

"No!" shouted a third voice, taking Zak completely by surprise. "I am not a child, that Jorum should go pleading to these men on my behalf. *Je suis un homme adulte!* I will not have it. *Jamais!*"

"Be silent, Rafe," growled the King. "Your recklessness last night put my son in danger – I will not hear any more excuses from you." King Edgar's voice rose in renewed anger. "You are a disgrace. My sister would be ashamed!"

"Sir, please hear me out," came the Chancellor's voice again. "Allow Prince Rafe to travel to London with your son. He will be under constant surveillance. He will not be in a position to misbehave. And when we return, I will deal with this problem."

There was a long, heavy silence, then Rafe's voice wafted out of the room.

"I do not wish to go to London," he said. "I have no interest in some infantile new computer game. Let Viktor go alone."

"Sir, trust me on this," said Jorum. "Prince Rafe should not be left here on his own. Send him to London. It will be for the best."

"I agree," growled the King. "Rafe – you will go to London, and you will behave as befits a Prince of the Royal line. And remember this – until you come of age, I have complete control over your finances. Unless you mend your ways, I will cut you off without a single Euro to your name."

"You cannot do that!" shouted Rafe.

"You will find that I can," said the King. "Do not put me to the test, Rafe. Nephew or not, I will cast you out if you disobey me again."

There was the sound of feet moving rapidly towards the door. Zak jumped back as Rafe stormed into the corridor. If the angry Prince had looked to the right, he would have seen Zak standing there pressed against the wall. Fortunately he didn't. He marched off in the opposite direction, emanating waves of resentment and rage as he went.

"The Prince will see sense once he calms down," said the Chancellor. "You have made a wise decision, Sir."

"I hope you are right, Chancellor," the King replied. "I am not easy in my mind about allowing the Crown Prince to accompany us to London. I was assured that British Intelligence would make the utmost effort to keep Viktor safe. So far, I am not impressed."

Not impressed. Zak had a sick feeling in the pit of his stomach.

"It was a simple error of judgment," said the Chancellor.

"But to send mere teenagers to protect my son!" insisted the King. "What are they thinking, Chancellor?"

"The boy did not let Viktor out of his sight, sir, remember that," said the Chancellor. "If not for the accident, all would have been well. I think you can trust him."

The King made an uncertain noise. "That is what Colonel Hunter said when we spoke last," he admitted. "He vouched for the boy." There was a pause. "Very well, we will do as you say. Rafe will come to London, and I will trust Colonel Hunter's agents to keep my son safe. You may go now, Chancellor."

Zak slipped away along the corridor and was around a corner before the Chancellor emerged.

So, Colonel Hunter had spoken up for him. Despite everything, the Colonel still had some faith in him.

Zak jogged back to his room.

He would do his best to make sure the Colonel's faith was well founded.

No more mistakes.

That was a promise.

The Royal Family had one last piece of official business to take care of before the trip to London. It was Queen Sophia's birthday, and magazines and TV networks had sent journalists and photographers from all over the world to secure interviews and to film and snap the Royals.

Chancellor Jorum showed the three Project 17 agents to the doorway of a very grand room decorated with mirrors and golden scrollwork. It was filled with a jostling crowd of photographers. The Queen was sitting in a plush chair at one end of the room, smiling radiantly, perfectly at ease in front of the cameras, dressed in a silk gown and wearing a silver tiara in her hair. King Edgar stood behind her, looking very regal in a navy blue uniform with gold buttons and brocade. Viktor was at her side, also in uniform. Zak was intrigued by the way the scruffy kid from last night had transformed himself into the solemn, stiff young heir to the throne again. Flashbulbs strobed and video cameras whirred.

He noticed Rafe was not there. He wondered whether the rebellious Prince had been told to stay away, or whether he was off sulking somewhere.

"There are interviews and photo shoots planned for the rest of the morning," Jorum told the three young agents as he led them away from the hectic room. "You will not be needed before lunchtime. A car can be arranged to take you to the town if you wish to do some sightseeing before you leave."

"That would be great, Sir," said Switchblade. "Thank you very much."

The Chancellor nodded and marched briskly away down the corridor.

Zak was relieved that the Chancellor hadn't said anything about last night. He might look grim and forbidding, but he seemed to be an okay sort of person. Zak had already told the other two what he'd overheard earlier that morning about Rafe's debts, and about his reluctance to go to London.

"He's obviously an idiot, but it's not our problem," Cat had said. "Let's keep an eye on him – just in case."

"Don't worry, I will," Zak had said. "And I'm not letting that lunatic anywhere near Viktor."

Switch had smiled. "A lesson learned, Silver."

Zak couldn't have agreed more. It was a lesson he wouldn't forget in a hurry.

A chauffeur-driven Bentley Mulsanne dropped them at the seafront and the three agents joined the throng of bronzed tourists wandering the streets of the old town. Every now and then the crowds would move aside as a gleaming sports car nosed its way through and went speeding off into the tangle of narrow streets and alleys behind the esplanades. The heat radiated off the roads, making the air shimmer. A host of competing scents wafted on the breeze. The tang of fresh fish, and ripe fruit from the open market stalls. The smell of hot tyre rubber on tarmac, and food being cooked in the seafront restaurants and cafés.

They made their way across a wide boulevard with manicured lawns and stone fountains, gazing at the ornate buildings with their stone sculptures and green copper roofs and old-world turrets.

After a while they found a café with outdoor tables and sat watching the people come and go from the grandiose hotels and shops. Cat took an endless stream of photos while Zak sucked a fruit juice through a straw. Switch was scrolling through his Mob, spouting facts about the history of Montevisto.

Zak gazed across the wide street at the rows of exclusive motor yachts lined up along the jetties of the marina, sleek and shiny and impossibly expensive. A little way out on the water, he could even see one massive yacht that had a helipad on the rear deck. How cool was that?

"Did you know that before 1850, most of this town was just a hillside covered in olive trees," Switch said. "It was King Edgar's great-great-great-grandfather who . . ."

"Look who it is!" said Zak, sitting up abruptly as a red open-top Ferrari came cruising along the esplanade, shining like a polished jewel. The car came to a stop and Prince Rafe climbed out, his eyes hidden behind sunshades.

"And all alone?" murmured Cat. "That's odd. I thought everyone in the Royal Family had a bodyguard or two when they went out in public."

"He's given his minders the slip, by the look of it," said Switch. "I call that very interesting."

All three agents were on the alert now, as the Prince walked briskly along the seafront.

"Nice wheels," murmured Cat. "A Ferrari F458 Italia Spider – the open-top version has only been on sale for a few months." She clicked her tongue. "Oh, to be rich!"

"Rafe looks as if he's in a hurry," said Zak, as the Prince pushed his way through the people wandering along the front.

"Places to go and people to see," said Switch. He felt in his pocket and drew out a small set of telescopic binoculars. Opening them up, he watched the Prince as he made his way rapidly along a jetty and up the gangplank of one of the largest of the yachts.

"Can you still see him?" asked Zak.

"Yes," said Switch, stretching up to his toes. "He's

shaking hands with a man on the yacht. Middle aged. Thinning, grey hair. Big belly. Really bad shirt and the worst shorts ever. Now they're going below."

"What's the name of the yacht?" asked Cat. "Can you see it?"

Switch ranged the binoculars over the stern. "Yes, it's called the *Goodfellow*."

Zak took out his Mob and tapped the little frog icon that would put him directly through to Bug.

"Hey, Bug," he said, as soon as the call was picked up. "We need help. Can you look up the name of the owner of a yacht called the *Goodfellow*."

There was silence.

Switch and Cat looked enquiringly at Zak. He shrugged, tapping the screen to put the call on speaker so the others could hear. "Bug? You there?"

"It's a Zeus Mangusta," came Bug's amplified voice. "Registered in Montevisto. Forty-nine point nine metres long, with a crew of eight and bunk space for twelve guests. Its cruising speed is twenty-four knots and if you want to make an offer on it, you'll need upwards of twenty-seven million Euros."

"You're a genius, Bug," said Zak. "Who owns it?"

"A guy by the name of Alfonso Gecko," said Bug. "Is that all?"

"That's all."

The line went dead. No goodbye. Bug really wasn't a phone person.

"Alfonso Gecko," said Zak. "Why do I know that name?"

Cat lowered her shades and looked at him. "You know it because he's the gangster boss Switch mentioned on the plane yesterday," she said. "Alfonso Gecko is one of the guys in the frame as the possible mastermind behind MARS."

CHAPTER **NINE**

"Crazy Prince Rafe meeting up with a big-time gangster," said Switch with a low whistle. "That can't be good."

"Didn't you say Gecko was involved with the casinos?" asked Wildcat. "What if it's Gecko that Rafe owes all the money to?"

"Don't gangsters get a bit cranky if they aren't paid back?" Zak looked uneasily at his two companions. "Like, *seriously* cranky?"

"Do you guys think it's a coincidence that Rafe's meeting up with Gecko the morning after he gets run off the road?" asked Cat. "I think maybe that *accident* last night was meant as a little reminder to Rafe that he needs to start paying up – or else."

Switch stared out over the marina. "And I don't like the idea of him meeting up with a guy who could be involved with MARS," he said. "I'd really like to know what's going on in that yacht."

"I could try to get closer," Zak suggested. "Sneak aboard and listen in, maybe?" *And make up for last night's disaster.*

"Without being noticed?" said Switch. "I don't think so."

Cat sat up sharply. "We could create a diversion," she said with a grin. "A piece of street theatre, so Silver could get onto the yacht unobserved." She looked at Switch. "Remember that circus routine we worked out when we were on Operation Big Top in Beijing last year?"

Switch nodded. "The acrobatics, yes," he said. "We were good, weren't we? It might just work."

Zak looked from one to the other. Operation Big Top? Beijing? That was in China. *Wow!* Working in Project 17 just never got old.

"Okay, here's the plan," said Switch. "Cat and I will go and perform alongside the *Goodfellow*." He nodded at Zak. "And while everyone's watching us, you find a way to get onboard the yacht. Don't take risks, okay? And if things turn bad, get out of there as quickly as you can. Got it?"

"Got it," said Zak. He stood up, gazing along the row of yachts lined up at the jetty. "And I know just what to do."

Zak watched as Switch and Cat walked along the jetty. The sleek white motor yachts bobbed on the water, moored by the sterns with their prows facing out into the Mediterranean. The huge one Zak had seen earlier was also there, at the far end – and now the helicopter was standing on the pad. The decks of the yachts were filled with suntanned people in swimming gear, lounging around drinking cocktails as if they didn't have a care in the world. Which they probably didn't, Zak assumed, if they could afford million-Euro yachts.

The two agents stopped in front of the *Goodfellow*. Zak kept his eyes on them, intrigued to see what they were planning to do. Without any preamble, Switch dropped to a crouch and Cat took his hands, lacing her fingers between his and bringing her feet up onto his bended knees. With an easy, fluid motion, she boosted herself into the air, kicking her legs up high. She wobbled for a moment as she found her balance, then she straightened her arms and stretched out, upside down, her toes pointing into the blue sky, her full weight supported on Switch's hands.

Zak watched, very impressed. He knew that Project 17 agents were super-fit, but this was something else.

Slowly, Switch straightened his legs until he was standing up, his arm muscles bulging as he took Wildcat's weight. Already, most of the people passing up and down the jetty had paused to watch, and even some of the people on the yachts were sitting up and taking notice.

Wildcat disengaged one hand and placed it on top of Switch's head, her legs spreading now as she realigned her balance. She took her other hand away and hung there inverted, supported by one hand on top of Switch's head as he slowly turned around, his arms stretching out to both sides.

There was applause and a few cheers as Wildcat opened her legs wider until she was doing the splits upside down. Then, moving very slowly, she brought her legs up together again, before shifting her grip so that her hands were now on Switch's shoulders. She flexed her arms and sprang up, turning a tight somersault before landing lightly and doing a neat little pirouette.

The two of them bowed as more applause rippled along the jetty.

Switch and Cat had hooked their audience, now it was time for Zak to get to work.

The *Goodfellow* was about the seventh or eighth yacht along in the tightly packed row. Zak made his way to the high, curved bow of the nearest yacht. He glanced around. No one seemed to have spotted him.

He stood poised for a moment on the stone lip of the walkway, then flexed his knees and jumped, snatching at the yacht's rail and bounding onto the deck. He looked towards the cabin. There was no one in sight. He stepped across the deck. The next yacht was moored no more than a metre away. He made the jump without any effort at all. Easy.

He heard another burst of applause and cheering from the jetty. He couldn't see Cat and Switch from here, but it sounded as though they were keeping the people nicely entertained.

He balanced for a moment on the edge of the second yacht's deck, then sprang across to the next. The deck was polished to a slippery sheen and Zak almost lost his balance, skidding as he landed.

Careful! You don't want to end up in the sea.

He ran across the yacht and launched himself off.

About two metres of open water stretched under him for a moment before his feet hit the next deck. This time he didn't pause. He sprinted over the deck and jumped again. Feet down. Run. Jump. Yacht to yacht. And so far, no one was even aware of him.

More clapping and cheering.

Keep it up, guys – I'm almost there.

The *Goodfellow* was the second largest yacht in the marina. It was a beautiful, luxurious craft, white as snow with black and silver trim and a chrome rail that ran around the high curved bows.

Zak sprang up, grasping the rail in both hands, and slid through onto the deck. He stood up, watchful and alert, ready to duck down again at the first sign of life. But there was no one on the sundeck, and no sight of any crew through the front window of the cabin.

He padded silently to the narrow walkway that ran alongside the cabin. The long, slim windows were tinted and it was hard to get a clear view of what was going on inside. Then he spotted a half-open window.

Keeping low, he moved closer. He could hear voices within. Hardly daring to breathe, he glided under the window, gradually lifting his head until his eyes were above the chrome sill.

Zak found himself staring into a large saloon cabin

with a polished wood floor and a ring of tan-coloured couches. Lamps and ornaments stood on side tables, and at one end there was a huge plasma-screen television.

Some kind of action movie was playing – all fast-cuts and red explosions and people being tossed through the air. But the sound had been muted and no one in the luxury cabin was watching.

Prince Rafe was perched on the edge of one of the couches, looking very uncomfortable – frightened, even. On either side of him sat a hefty, blank-faced man. Both men had shaved heads and wore sunglasses and dark suits. Their thighs and biceps strained against the material, as if their muscular bodies were too big for normal clothing. Dangerous, Zak thought, like two Rottweilers waiting to be let off the leash. One of the men was reading a magazine. The other was bent over a low table, shuffling and cutting a pack of cards over and over.

A fat man in a floral-design Hawaiian shirt and canvas shorts was lounging on the couch facing the Prince, a glass in one hand and a cigar in the other. He was obviously the man Switch had seen through the binoculars. Despite his bad clothes he seemed to be in absolute control – as if he was so powerful that it didn't matter how he was dressed.

Alfonso Gecko, Zak assumed. The Montevisto gang lord in person.

"Well?" asked the man. His accent was thick and sounded Eastern European. "I do not have all day, Rafe. What is your decision?"

Rafe stared at him – and now Zak could see that the Prince was definitely scared. "I . . . I . . . do not know . . ." he stammered. "*Il est difficile.* It is difficult."

Alfonso Gecko's voice purred, but it was heavy with menace. "Perhaps Bruno and Max could help you make your mind up? I have only to ask them. They are – how do you say it? – most obliging. Bruno has certain useful skills." He gestured first to the man with the magazine, then to the card player. "And Max can be extremely persuasive."

Rafe looked from side to side in some alarm, but the man on his left just kept flicking through the magazine while the other one shuffled and cut, shuffled and cut as if he wasn't even listening.

Zak could guess the kind of help the two thugs would be asked to dish out.

"I will do it," Rafe said slowly. He let out a low groan. "You give me no choice."

"Excellent," said Alfonso Gecko. "Then we need

detain you no longer, Rafe."

The Prince got up and walked rapidly to the rear of the cabin.

"But remember this, Your Royal Highness," Alfonso Gecko called. "If you do not do as we ask, the next time we meet I will not be so friendly. If you love life, do not fail me."

Rafe glanced back at him, and Zak saw the sweat running down his face. He said nothing and a few moments later he left the cabin.

Alfonso Gecko took a swig from his glass and said something in a foreign language. The two men laughed.

Zak was annoyed with himself. If he'd been a bit quicker off the mark, he might have got to the window in time to find out what it was that Rafe had been forced to do.

As it was, all he knew for sure was that Alfonso Gecko had put the frighteners on the Prince – and it seemed to have worked.

Time to go.

He turned, intending to make his way to the front of the boat again and yacht-hop back to land. But his foot slipped and he dropped heavily onto his knees with a stifled yelp of pain.

He heard a sharp word of command from inside,

followed by the clatter of heavy feet across the wooden floor.

He'd been heard! Gecko was sending his two heavies to investigate.

Zak shot a glance to the front of the yacht. Did he have time to go that way? Maybe – and he could probably outrun those two goons even if they did spot him. But that wasn't the point. The point was that they should not see him at all. Covert surveillance doesn't really work if you get seen.

He stayed low, his heart pounding as he considered his options. He heard a hatch open at the front of the yacht. One of the men appeared, dark against the clear blue sky, shaved head shining in the sunlight. Zak heard the other man moving about in the stern. Another few moments and they'd be coming at him from both sides.

His options were narrowing down. He crawled to the bow and peered into the smooth clear water – so clear that he could see the pebbles and sand at the bottom. No choice. He slid around and lowered himself feet first over the side. Don't make a splash! Don't let them know there was ever anyone here.

He stretched to the full extent of his arms, then let go, dropping into the water and feeling it swirl warmly around him. His feet touched the bottom and he pushed up again, lifting his hands to prevent himself from cracking his head on the hull of the boat.

He broke the surface, treading water, hidden under the deep curve of the yacht. He heard voices above him for a few moments, then the voices faded. Bruno and Max were giving up.

Zak swam for the jetty. He had info now that Switch and Cat would be very interested to hear.

They were in Wildcat's room at the Palace, video linked to Colonel Hunter at Fortress.

"You have no idea what Prince Rafe agreed to?" the Colonel asked when Zak finished his report. "No clue at all?"

"All I know is that he really didn't want to do it," said Zak. "Gecko had to threaten to set the two heavies on him before he gave in."

The Colonel's expression was thoughtful. "At the moment, we don't have enough information to act on what Quicksilver saw," he said at last. "Gecko is obviously using Prince Rafe's debts to put pressure on him about something. We need to keep Rafe on a tight lead. I want you to watch him closely, but don't spook him." There was a brief pause as he considered his next words. "Interpol have been trying to put Alfonso Gecko behind bars for ten years now. He's a slippery customer. If this business with Rafe helps convict him, we'll have done a good day's work."

"Are you concerned that this might have something to do with MARS, Control?" asked Switchblade. "According to what I read, Gecko is in the frame as the possible brains behind the whole organization."

"Him and half a dozen others," said the Colonel. "I find it hard to believe that Prince Rafe would agree to do anything that would jeopardize the lives of the Royal Family. You've seen him up close. Does he seem capable of letting them come to harm to save himself?"

"Tricky to say," said Switch.

"I can't see it myself," added Wildcat. "He's a bit of an idiot, but that's all."

"I agree with Cat," said Zak. "He's really full of himself and he thinks he's the smartest guy on the planet, but he likes Prince Viktor – I don't think he'd want MARS to blow him up. No way."

"Then keep your eyes peeled, and report back if you see anything suspicious," said Colonel Hunter. "What time is your flight out of there?"

"We'll be flying out in a private charter with Prince Viktor at fifteen hundred hours local time," said Wildcat.

"If everything runs to schedule, we'll be landing at Heathrow . . ." She paused for a moment to consult her Mob. ". . . At approximately fifteen forty-five UK time. The King and Queen and Prince Rafe will be on the next flight. Apparently they don't like the King and the Crown Prince to travel in the same aeroplane."

"That's in case of an accident or a terrorist attack on the plane," said the Colonel. "Our Royals have the same protocol. Rooms have been booked for the royal party at the Berwick Hotel in Soho. If nothing happens in the meantime, contact me again when you arrive there." The Colonel gave a curt nod and cut the line.

The three agents looked at one another.

"Well, we have our orders," said Switch, getting up. "Time to get packed."

"And if there's a MARS bomb on the plane?" asked Zak, only half-joking.

"You know the routine," said Wildcat. "Get between Prince Viktor and the explosion."

"Oh, nice," said Zak. "That's a comforting thought."

Switch smiled grimly. "Who told you being in Project 17 was going to be comfortable?" he asked.

Good point.

Nobody had.

CHAPTER **TEN**

Montevisto International Airport was on special alert as the convoy of limousines arrived mid-afternoon, carrying Zak and Wildcat and Switchblade, along with Prince Viktor and Chancellor Jorum and about a dozen agents of royal security.

They were ushered quickly to the VIP lounge, where Zak spotted men in black uniforms with automatic weapons slung over their shoulders. Clearly, no chances were being taken with the Prince's safety.

Prince Viktor was in "royal mode", as Zak had come to think of it: solemn and formal. But Zak was beginning to catch on: Viktor only behaved like this in front of other people. It was expected of him. Zak wondered what it must be like to have to play the part of the Crown Prince for so much of the time. He knew it would drive him round the bend.

He walked over to where the Prince was sitting, gazing out of the huge windows at the taxiing aeroplanes and the baggage trucks.

He sat down. The Prince glanced at him. "Is everything on schedule?" he asked.

"I think so," Zak replied.

Viktor gave him a long, slow look. "I'm expected to behave in a certain way," he said, as though he'd been reading Zak's thoughts. He gestured to where the Chancellor was standing with a group of security guards. "I play the game. I don't really have a choice. My father would be upset if he thought I was letting the House of Corvetti down." A smile stole over his face. "When I'm King, I'm going to demolish the Palace and set up a bouncy castle on the hilltop instead."

Zak grinned. "Sounds like an idea," he said.

An airport official came up to the Prince and bowed. "Everything is ready for you to board now, Your Highness," he said.

The Prince stood up and nodded. "Thank you," he

said, beckoning to Zak to follow as he marched towards the departure gate.

"Next stop, London," said Zak. He looked at the Prince. "Have you ever been to London?"

"Yes, just once," said Viktor as they headed along the enclosed walkway to the waiting aeroplane. "I didn't get time for much sightseeing though. We stayed at Buckingham Palace. The private guest apartments are really quite pleasant. Have you seen them?"

"Not as such," said Zak, following the Prince into the aeroplane. "I don't get that many invites to the Palace."

Viktor insisted that Zak sit next to him. Wildcat and Switchblade were behind, and just across the aisle, the Chancellor was seated with his table down, working on some documents.

Viktor spent a lot of time during the flight retrieving images of dinosaurs on his smartphone and getting Zak to guess their names. Zak got about half of them right. Viktor knew them all.

Zak's Mob made a croaking noise.

Incoming from Bug.

On a normal flight, they wouldn't have had access, but on the Prince's private jet, it was no problem.

Zak tapped the screen and a text message popped up.

More chatter picked up from MARS. This just in from MI5 surveillance. Message reads: The Great Moment Approaches! When The Tyrant King Speaks, His Roar Will Bring Death To The House Of Corvetti.

"What's the message?" asked Viktor. "Anything important?"

Zak cleared the screen. "Not really," he said. "Just an update." He glanced over his shoulder to where Cat and Switch were sitting. They were also looking at their Mobs. They'd received the same message.

Switch nodded to Viktor then shook his head. He was obviously thinking the same as Zak – there was no point in freaking the Prince out.

Zak settled back in his seat. An ominous feeling crept over him.

How much danger were they flying into?

Switchblade was waiting by the walk-through metal detector at the entrance of the VIP arrivals lounge in Heathrow Airport. The others from Flight MI756 had already travelled on to the hotel where the Royal Family would be staying, but Colonel Hunter had given Switch a special task to perform.

A courier had been waiting for him with a parcel.

It contained an exact replica of Prince Rafe's mobile phone – with a small addition. A hidden app that Bug had designed. It would allow them to listen to any calls Rafe made as well as pinpoint his location via GPS whether the phone was operative or not.

Switchblade's job was to wait by the scanner. When the Prince put his coins and keys and other metal objects in the tray, he was to sneak the phone off and plug it and the replica into a special little device that would clone everything on the Prince's phone in less than thirty seconds. The security guards had been instructed to keep the Prince busy with the body scanner while he did this. Then Switch would slip the cloned phone into the tray without the Prince even noticing.

He moved out of sight behind the scanning machinery as he saw the royal party approaching. Rafe was in the lead, looking ill humoured and sour faced. He piled his metal and electronic belongings into the tray and walked through the detector. There was a loud beep. Rafe was asked to walk through again. Beep. Apologizing, the security guards used up a few moments running hand-held metal detectors over him. When Switch gave them the nod, they let the Prince through.

Switch watched from cover as the sulky Prince pocketed his replica phone, then he turned and slipped quietly away.

He smiled to himself as he jogged down the back stairs to meet the driver of the motorbike that was waiting for him. Job done. Job very nicely done.

The penthouse suites of the Berwick Hotel took up the whole of the top floor, and all five of the suits had been assigned to the Royal Family of Montevisto. About an hour after Prince Viktor and the Chancellor checked in, the other Royals arrived without incident. So far, everything seemed to be going smoothly.

Zak and Viktor stood on the balcony of the Prince's suite in the late afternoon sunlight, gazing out over a panorama of London. The balcony faced south, and across the rooftops they could see the towers of the Houses of Parliament and the high curve of the London Eye. Behind them was the huge main room with its king-size bed and a wide reception area where couches and armchairs gathered around a low table.

"So, does this come up to the standards of Buckingham Palace?" asked Zak, hooking his thumb over his shoulder to indicate the suite.

"I like that it's modern," said Viktor. "You can get sick of old-fashioned stuff."

"So, living in a castle isn't all it's cracked up to be?" Zak said with a smile.

"I'd swap with you in a heartbeat," said Viktor. Zak wasn't quite sure how serious that was. "What's it like working for British Intelligence?" asked the Prince. "Tell me about some of the missions you've been on."

"I can't do that," Zak said.

"Is it classified?" asked Viktor.

Zak paused. Should he tell the truth? Or would it be better to let Viktor think he was more experienced?

"Actually, this is my first mission," Zak admitted.

The Prince gave him a surprised look. "Oh." He sounded a little disappointed. "I suppose everyone's got to start somewhere. You're fully trained, though, aren't you? You know plenty of ways to kill anyone who attacks me?"

Zak raised his eyebrows. "How many ways do I need to know?" he asked.

Viktor smiled. "I suppose one would do," he said.

"We're not actually trained to kill people," Zak explained. "But I know how to take someone down if I need to. I've done a course in unarmed combat. You know – martial arts, like Brazilian jiu-jitsu and Krav Maga and wing chun."

Viktor's eyes widened. "Show me," he said, stepping through the glass doors and turning around on the thick-pile carpet with his arms spread out. "Do some on me."

Zak eyed him dubiously, weighing up the consequences. *Um, sorry, Your Majesty, don't get mad, but I kind of broke your son's neck while I was showing him the palm-heel-strike to the chin.*

Zak's Mob chimed out Switch's melody before he needed to decide what to do.

"I'm in with Cat," came Switchblade's voice. "Hunter's on video. He wants you right now."

"I have to go," Zak said in some relief as he headed for the door. "Duty calls."

When The Tyrant King Speaks, His Roar Will Bring Death To The House Of Corvetti.

"Does MI5 think MARS is planning to blow the King up while he's giving his speech to the conference?" asked Wildcat.

She, Switch and Zak were in another of the penthouse suites in the Berwick Hotel, linked via video to Colonel Hunter in Fortress. Everything was still on schedule. The King and Queen had been whisked away under MI5 protection for a live interview at BBC Television Centre.

Chancellor Jorum was in Whitehall, having a meeting with some officials from the British Government and Prince Rafe was in his suite – probably grinding his teeth and wishing he was back home, Zak guessed.

"An attack at the climate summit is certainly one interpretation of the message," agreed the Colonel. "But MI5 have swept the conference centre for explosive devices, and they haven't found anything."

"What if one of the delegates has a bomb strapped to themselves?" asked Switch. "How easy would it be for them to just walk up to the King, shake his hand and go *boom*?"

"MI5 says the security at the conference centre is airtight," said the Colonel. "They have detectors on every entrance, plus anyone entering the venue will be searched, and all bags, shoes and coats will be subject to a CTX imaging scan."

"Has the hotel been thoroughly searched?" asked Zak.

"Several times," the Colonel replied. "And specially trained sniffer dogs are being used to find any explosives."

"What about staff background checks?" asked Wildcat.

"Everyone's been vetted twice," said Colonel Hunter. He started suddenly, as if he'd been jabbed by a needle.

He put a hand to the Bluetooth at his right ear. "Say that again," he snapped.

Zak, Switch and Wildcat stared at one another. Clearly, some significant piece of intelligence had just been passed to the Colonel.

"Yes. Got it. We're on it." He stared out of the computer screen. "Prince Rafe is missing from his hotel suite," he barked. "This is what we've been waiting for. Switchblade, Wildcat – you're on him. Arm's length surveillance. Keep it eyes-on if you can, but if he seems suspicious, lose visual contact rather than let him see you."

"Game on, Control," said Switch, as he and Wildcat jumped up.

"Keep in constant contact," said the Colonel. "Remember, there are potential killers out there. Don't take any chances. Be smart. Be safe."

"What should I do, Control?" asked Zak.

"Stay with Prince Viktor," said Colonel Hunter. "Don't let him out of your sight."

Switchblade and Wildcat ran to the lift. Wildcat was activating the surveillance tech app on her Mob even as Switch stabbed at the ground floor button.

"Got him?" Switch asked as the lift descended.

Wildcat smiled. "Oh, yes," she said. She showed Switchblade the screen. A close-up GPS street map was displayed. A red dot pulsed regularly. "He's not gone far," she said. "A few streets away. And he's not moving."

"Let's go and see what he's up to," said Switch as the lift's doors opened. They ran across the hotel's lavish reception area and out into the street.

Prince Rafe wasn't hard to find. The two agents spotted him sitting in the window of a café in a busy, touristy side street. There was a cup on the table in front of him, but he wasn't drinking. A black leather shoulder bag hung from the back of his chair. The Prince was biting his nails and peering up and down the street.

"He looks nervous," Cat said as they watched from the corner of the street. "There's no way he's come here for a cup of coffee."

Switchblade touched the screen of his Mob and held it to his ear. "Control?" he said. "We have him. He's alone but we think he's going to meet someone. Watch and wait? Yes, that's exactly what we're planning to do."

"What's happened?" asked Viktor as he let Zak back into his suite. "I heard some people running about a minute or two ago, but everything's gone quiet again." He held up his mobile phone. "I tried calling Rafe, but he's not answering."

"It's nothing," said Zak as he closed the door behind him. "Everything's under control." He flipped the lock, trying to make it look casual. He walked across to the plasma-screen TV and picked up the remote. "Do you want to watch something?"

"I've brought my Wii games console," said Viktor. "There's a new version of Dino-Hunter due out in a few months." He grinned. "I've got an advance copy. It's pretty cool. We could play that."

"Sounds good to me," said Zak.

"And I've called room service," Viktor added. "They're bringing up some pizza. There'll be enough for both of us."

"Great," said Zak.

They were midway through the game when a knock sounded.

"It's the pizza," said Viktor, jumping up and running for the door. "About time. I'm starving."

"Wait! Let me get that," said Zak, scrambling to his feet. What was he thinking? What kind of bodyguard lets the person they're meant to be protecting answer the door?

But by the time he caught up with the Prince, Viktor had already unlocked the door and pulled it open.

Two men in hotel staff uniforms of white shirts and waistcoats stood there with a food trolley. They had shaved heads and bodies that seemed too big and muscular for normal clothes.

Zak recognized them in a single horrifying instant.

Alfonso Gecko's heavies from the yacht.

He gave a yell and snatched at Viktor's collar, dragging him back. He tried to slam the door, but the man called Bruno shoved the trolley forwards, barging the door wide, while the other one, Max, pulled a gun out of his belt and aimed it at Prince Viktor's head.

CHAPTER **ELEVEN**

Zak raised his hands and backed away as the two men moved into the room. The handgun had a silencer screwed onto its muzzle. This was a disaster. He hadn't been prepared – and now the Crown Prince might pay for his carelessness with his life.

The trolley was shoved aside and Bruno closed the door behind them.

"If you harm me, my father will hunt you down to the ends of the world," Viktor said as Max pushed him further into the room. Zak was impressed at the Prince's bravery, but this wasn't a good time to get mouthy.

"No harm will come to you if you do exactly as you are told," said Max. He had the same kind of Eastern European accent as Gecko. He gestured with the gun. "If you have mobile phones, throw them onto the floor," he demanded.

"I don't take orders from scum like you," retorted Viktor. "Shoot me if you must, I'm not afraid of you."

A cold smile twitched at one side of the gunman's mouth. He swung his arm, aiming the gun at Zak. "I will not shoot you, Prince Viktor," he said between gritted teeth. "You are too valuable to us alive. But I will shoot this boy if you defy us." His eyes glittered with menace. "Do I need to convince you that I speak the truth?"

Viktor hesitated for a moment then put his hand in his pocket and threw his mobile phone to the floor.

Bruno stepped forwards, shoving Zak up against the wall and frisking him with big, powerful hands. He found the Mob. He showed it to Max and said something in a foreign language. The gunman replied briefly, shaking his head. Bruno dropped the Mob and stamped down hard on it two or three times. Then he picked up both of the phones and took them into the bathroom. Zak heard water running into the basin. Even the Mob couldn't survive that kind of treatment.

"Listen very carefully to me," Max said to the Prince.

"You will do exactly as I tell you. If you try to escape or raise the alarm, I will shoot your friend, do you understand?"

"I understand," Viktor said calmly.

Zak's mind was racing. How was he going to get them out of this? Even without the gun, he knew he probably didn't have the power or the skills to take down both of these men. His only option seemed to be to do as they asked and hope they were missed quickly enough for a rescue to be organized.

The timing of this attack had been well thought out, Zak realized – the MI5 teams were with the King and Queen and the Chancellor. Switch and Wildcat were hunting for Rafe. Security was at its most lax right now. There was only Agent Quicksilver – and he was useless.

A horrible thought struck him – was this what Rafe had agreed to do for Gecko? To go missing and lure the agents away so that Bruno and Max would have the perfect opportunity to snatch his cousin? Was Rafe *that* desperate?

"Tie them up," Max barked. Bruno took some thin plastic ties out of his pocket and used them to bind Zak and the Prince's wrists behind their backs. Gags were pushed into their mouths.

Zak looked anxiously at the Prince, wishing he could reassure him. Viktor stared back at him levelly. Zak could see the fear in his eyes. The Prince was not prepared to show it in front of the two thugs, but he was terrified.

It occurred to Zak that this would be the perfect moment for him to use Code Winter. Except that he had no one to tell and no way of telling them.

Max opened the door and looked into the corridor.

"All clear," he said, moving out and gesturing with his gun.

Bruno pushed Zak and the Prince into the hallway. A large plastic container stood against the wall. Bruno lifted the lid and Zak saw rumpled sheets inside. A laundry basket.

Zak and Viktor were bundled roughly into the basket and the lid was closed on them. They lay pressed back to back in the gloom as the basket was wheeled along the hall.

Zak strained his wrists against the plastic ties, but he quickly gave up – it hurt too much and he knew it was futile. He needed to conserve his energy. Wait and see.

The basket juddered and became still. Zak heard a soft ping and the hiss of closing automatic doors. They were in a lift. A few moments passed. Zak was finding it hard to concentrate on what was happening outside the basket – blood was pounding so loudly in his head that he could hardly hear anything else.

The lift stopped and the basket was pushed along for a while.

Where were they going? And what would happen to them when they got there?

The sounds changed suddenly and the light filtering in around the edges of the lid grew brighter. They were outside now. There were clanking noises and then the feeling that the basket was being lifted. It was pushed again. It came to a sudden bone-shaking stop. A few seconds later there was a metallic clattering sound and the light dimmed again. Zak heard muffled voices at a distance. Where were they?

Then he heard the low growl of an engine starting. The floor vibrated under them. Got it! They were in the back of a truck.

But why had the Prince been kidnapped? If the plan was to kill King Edgar, where did the abduction of Prince Viktor fit into the scheme?

Escape first. Figure it all out later, okay?

Zak held his breath, listening intently. He could hear nothing other than the guttural growl of the motor and the echoing rattle as the truck moved off.

Were they alone in the back?

He hoped so.

Time to get busy.

He squirmed in the confines of the basket, trying to find room enough to draw his feet up behind himself. He felt the Prince move, and heard a muffled grunt from him.

Sorry, thought Zak, as he kicked Viktor in the back. *It'll be worth it. Just wait!* He strained with his hands. The plastic tie cut into his flesh. Painful, but he had to do this. He groped downwards with his fingers, arching himself, trying to bring his feet up higher.

His fingers made contact with his shoes. He felt blindly around the heel of his right shoe. There was a small trigger point under the instep. He jerked at it with a fingertip and felt the heel come loose. Fighting to get a grip, he twisted it around. He pushed his fingers into the cavity, wincing as his fingertip grazed across a sharp, serrated edge.

Trying to ignore the unnatural tension on his muscles and joints, Zak tweaked at the wound-up length of flexible saw blade until it came loose. It slipped out of his fingers and for a panicky moment he had to grope for it among the creases and folds of the bed sheets before he located it again.

The Prince was bumping up against him now, making incoherent grunting noises through his gag.

Calm down! thought Zak. *Give me a minute.*

He closed his eyes, concentrating. He angled the thin blade so that its cutting edge was pressing against the plastic tie. He began to saw. Every now and then the truck would shudder to a halt or go over some uneven piece of road or turn a sudden corner, throwing Zak off. But slowly, gradually, he cut into the tie until, ignoring the pain gnawing into his wrists, he managed to snap it.

He twisted around, bringing his aching arms forwards and drawing his hands up to his mouth. He pulled out the gag. He gasped and let out a long breath.

"Viktor?" he whispered. "I'm free. Stay still. Keep quiet – in case there's someone in here with us."

The Prince lay unmoving while Zak pulled the gag out of his mouth and got to work on the plastic tie.

"How did you get free?" whispered the Prince.

"Secret agent stuff," murmured Zak. "I'll show you later."

"We're in some kind of vehicle," hissed the Prince. "Where do you think they're taking us?"

"How should I know?" Zak said. "Shut up so I can concentrate on what I'm doing."

It didn't take long to hack through the Prince's bonds. Then Zak got to his knees, crouching under the lid of the basket. Very slowly he raised the lid, peering cautiously through the gap. It was dark in the back of the truck, but there was enough light for him to see that they were alone.

"Don't make a noise," Zak hissed in Viktor's ear.

Quietly and carefully, the two of them climbed out of the laundry basket.

Zak sat down for a moment, winding the saw blade up again and fitting it back into his shoe. He clicked the heel into place.

"Very resourceful," Viktor whispered. "What's in the other heel? Some kind of device to cut through metal, I hope?"

"Not exactly," Zak said. He moved to the back of the truck. A metal shutter was drawn down. He tried to get his fingers under it.

He pulled hard but the shutter didn't budge. "Locked," he said.

He had hoped that they might be able to leap out of the truck as it waited at a set of lights or got held up in traffic. But that wasn't an option with a locked steel shutter standing between them and freedom.

"We'll have to wait till they unlock the back," he told the Prince. "Then we need to take them by surprise and get away before they know what's happening."

"Okay," said the Prince. "How do we do that?"

"Let's push the laundry basket up to the shutter," Zak

said, thinking quickly. "We get behind it and when they pull the shutter up we shove it right in their faces. And while they're flat out, we leg it." He gave Viktor a hard look. "You have to find the nearest escape route, and just go for it. Do you understand?"

Viktor nodded. "Yes, we run." He shrugged. "It's not difficult to understand."

"No," said Zak. "I mean, you don't look back. You don't wait for me. You don't worry about me at all. You just *run*." His eyes bored into Viktor's. "Now do you understand?"

Viktor's eyes narrowed. "I see," he said. "You mean, I should save myself – even if it means leaving you behind."

Zak nodded.

The Prince shook his head. "I'm not going to do that," he said. "We'll get out together."

"I'm supposed to be protecting you," said Zak vehemently. "I've made a total mess of it so far. You have to get away from these people."

The Prince smiled. "Together or nothing," he said firmly. "Who's the Prince around here? You'll do as I tell you."

"Or you'll have me beheaded?" Zak said.

"Absolutely, I will."

Zak sighed. "Okay," he agreed. "Together or nothing."

*

The truck came to a halt, its engine still running. Zak and the Prince looked at one another. They had positioned the laundry basket sideways up close to the shutter and they were sitting on the floor behind it.

Waiting.

The truck started again and moved forwards. The light from outside dimmed.

"We're in a building," Zak said.

Viktor nodded, swallowing hard. Zak looked at him. His fists were balled up in his lap.

"This is going to be really easy," Zak told him. "They won't know what's hit them. We'll be out of here in ten seconds flat."

Viktor nodded again, trying to smile.

The truck stopped and the engine cut out.

This was it. Zak stood up, balancing himself, getting a firm grip on the edge of the laundry basket. Viktor was poised at his side.

Push. Jump. Run.

Easy.

There were voices at the back of the truck. The shutter began to clank noisily upwards. Light spilled in.

"Now!" Zak yelled. Digging in hard with his feet, he threw his full weight against the laundry basket. It skidded over the edge. Zak saw Max's startled face, his mouth open. A split second later, Max's face along with the rest of him vanished under the toppling basket.

Bruno jumped back, but he caught his heel on something and crashed to the ground.

"Go! Go! Go!" Zak shouted as he sprang out of the truck, vaulting easily over the basket while Max sprawled underneath it. Viktor jumped with him, but he landed awkwardly and staggered, his arms flailing as he tried to keep his balance.

Zak only had a moment to take in their surroundings. They were in a large warehouse. He spotted a concrete stairway leading up to swing doors. That was their way out.

He was halfway across the floor before he realized Viktor wasn't with him. He turned, his heart pounding. Viktor was on the ground – Bruno was holding his ankle and dragging him back.

Zak ran back to the Prince. But before he could get to him, the laundry basket tipped aside and suddenly Max was there with his gun, a murderous grimace on his face.

Zak stopped dead, lifting his hands. Alone, he might have tried to jump the gunman and hope for the best. Now he had to think of the Prince. Bruno's arm was crooked around Viktor's neck in a vice-like grip. The two thugs might have orders to keep the Prince alive for now – but that wouldn't stop them hurting him.

Max strode towards Zak, raising his gun arm. Zak winced, expecting a blow. But a crooked smile came over Max's face and he brought his other beefy hand up to pat Zak's cheek. "You try to help your friend," he growled. "I can respect that." He pressed the muzzle of the gun into Zak's forehead. "Do it again, I kill you. No more warning. Understand?"

Zak nodded.

Viktor and Bruno were on their feet.

"I'm sorry," Viktor called. "I let you down."

"No, you didn't," said Zak.

Max dug his fingers into Zak's shoulder and marched him across the floor. "Friendship is good," he said. "Friends comfort one another in times of trouble. It is good. I like that."

He led Zak to the folding metal gate of a freight lift. Pushing the gun into his belt, he jerked the gate open. There was no lift. Zak stared down the shaft. A hard push in the middle of his back sent him staggering forwards. He tottered for a moment then fell.

The drop was about five metres onto a heap of sacking. The landing jarred his knees and knocked the breath out of him. He got to his feet and looked up just as Viktor was pushed over the edge. He tried to break the Prince's fall, and they both went crashing down onto the sacks.

There was a rattle as the metal gate was closed above them.

Echoing footsteps receded.

"Are you okay?" Zak asked the Prince.

Viktor pushed his hair out off his eyes. He nodded. "Now what?" he asked, his voice shaking.

"I don't know," Zak said, despair beginning to take hold. "I haven't the faintest idea, *okay*?"

So far, nothing he'd tried had worked. There was a metal gate at this level, but it was padlocked and the basement room beyond was dark. A sudden anger boiled up in him and he lashed out, punching the cement wall. The pain burned through him, shocking him. He sucked his raw knuckles, tasting blood.

Viktor eyed him uneasily but said nothing.

What was there to say?

"How long has he been gone?" asked Switch. They were still at the same corner, watching the café. A few minutes ago, Prince Rafe had got up from his table. But he had not come out onto the street. They'd assumed he was using the toilets.

But then two minutes became five, and they began to wonder.

Wildcat was looking intently at her Mob. "He hasn't moved," she said. "He's still in there."

Switchblade stared across the street. A young man and woman entered the café and were shown to Rafe's table. His mug was taken away. That was when Switch noticed that the black leather bag was also gone.

"I don't like this," he said. "I'm going in. Stay here, in case he makes a run for it."

Switch marched across the street and went into the café. He looked around, wondering whether Rafe had taken a different table. He wasn't there. Switch walked to the back and pushed through a swing door into the toilets.

The mobile phone lay in one of the basins. Switchblade recognized it immediately. He snatched it up and ran back into the corridor. A back door was open a fraction. He walked into a small cluttered yard with a wooden fence. The door out of the yard was also open.

Spitting a curse, Switch called Wildcat on her Mob.

"He's gone!" he said as he ran into an alley. "He's

smarter than we thought – or someone's giving him good advice."

"There's worse," came Wildcat's strained voice. "Control just called. Viktor and Quicksilver are missing."

Zak stood on Viktor's shoulders, but even if he stretched his arms up as far as he could, there was no way of reaching the floor above. He stared up in frustration. It was hopeless. Pointless.

He was about to tell Viktor that he was coming down again when he heard a voice. It was some way off, and Zak had to really strain to hear what was being said. It was Max – and he seemed to be talking on a phone.

"Yes, we have him," he was saying. "Safe and secure. But the plan has changed. We want twice the amount of ransom we agreed." There was a pause. "No, you listen to me. If we do not receive the money in six hours, we will start to send the little Prince back to his parents in small sections – do you understand me?" Another pause. "Yes, I know this was not our agreement, but if you wish to run with the wolves, you must learn to obey the rules of the pack. Do as I tell you – send our demands off immediately, or we start cutting off royal body parts."

There was silence, then Zak heard the two men speaking together in their own language.

He lowered himself slowly and Viktor helped him jump down.

"I heard voices," said the Prince. "Did you hear what they were saying?"

Zak shook his head. Viktor didn't need to know what the thugs had planned for him. "They were talking Russian or something like that," he said.

Sometimes, it was better to be economical with the truth.

CHAPTER **TWELVE**

FORTRESS. BUG'S HIGH-TECH OFFICE.

Bug tapped rapidly at his keyboard. Colonel Hunter was standing behind him, reading the final lines of an email enlarged on a plasma screen.

. . . ransom of £5,000,000, or Prince Viktor will be returned piece by piece. You have fifteen minutes to respond to this, and six hours to gather the money. That is all. There will be no further contact.

"And when did you intercept this message?" asked Hunter.

"It was sent to King Edgar's smartphone five minutes ago," Bug said.

"There's no mention of a second kidnapped boy," said the Colonel. "No word on Agent Quicksilver."

"He wasn't at the hotel," Bug said. "So he must have been taken. His Mob was there, but it had been disabled."

Colonel Hunter's fingers gripped the back of Bug's chair. "Can you trace the origin of the email?" he said.

"The MI5 agents are already working on it," Bug said, his fingers flying over the keyboard. "But none of them are as good as me." A world map appeared on screen. A blue dot pulsed over London.

"No," Colonel Hunter said quietly. "They're not, Bug. You're the best."

Bug typed again. A line spun out towards Europe. "This guy is also very good," he said as the line bent suddenly and went streaking away eastwards. "He's routed the email through Geneva and Kuala Lumpur." The line streaked off the map and appeared again on the other side. "Los Angeles," breathed Bug, blowing his cheeks out. The line raced east again. "Moscow," said Bug, still typing. "Addis Ababa." He glanced up at Colonel Hunter's strained face. "He's all over the map, Control," he said. "This could take a while."

"Keep on it, Bug," said the Colonel. "I'm going to liaise

with MI5. The King will have to respond to the kidnappers in the next few minutes. Let me know the second you have anything." The door slammed and Bug was alone in his room. Frowning over his keyboard, Bug continued the worldwide game of chase-the-email. Except it was no game. If he didn't get this right, Quicksilver and the Crown Prince would end up dead.

"This is hopeless," said Zak, sitting back and flexing his numbed fingers. "It's not going to work." He'd been frantically sawing at the padlock that held the lower grill closed. The thin flexible blade was having little effect, and his fingers were cramped and sore from the effort.

"Let me try," said the Prince.

"It's no good," replied Zak. "It's not even cutting it, and the blade is just getting blunter and blunter." He guessed that it had never been intended to work on hardened steel.

Zak stood up, stretching his limbs, wondering how long they had already been down there. All was silent above.

Zak stared up the lift shaft. In the shadows he could see dangling loops of metal cable and the underside of the lift.

I hope no one decides to use the lift to get to the basement, he thought. *We'd be squashed like . . .*

He decided not to finish that thought.

"We could tear these pieces of sacking into strips," Viktor suggested. "If we threw them up, one end might catch on the gate."

"We'd need a hook for that to work," Zak said.

They spent a few futile minutes throwing the sacking around, hoping to find something useful underneath. They didn't.

Zak leaned against the back wall of the shaft, staring up at the gate again. Five metres wasn't such a stretch if he was in the zone. But he couldn't conjure the zone out of thin air. It took time. It took effort and concentration.

"Listen," he said, "I want to try something. It may not work, and it's going to look weird." He frowned. How to explain? "I need to run for a while, okay? Then, when I give the word, I need you to help boost me up." He pointed at the gate. "To that."

"We've already tried that," Viktor pointed out.

"Not this way we haven't."

Zak grabbed all the sacking and piled it in one corner, out of the way. He began to jog around the Prince, running a tight circle around him, pumping his arms, his eyes half-closed to help him focus.

The Prince watched him. Puzzled but saying nothing.

Zak sped up, the circle widening so he was grazing the four walls of the shaft with his shoulder.

Come on, zone, don't fail me now.

Faster. Fending off the walls with his arm now, his forearm and hand bruised by the rhythmic impact of the concrete. Round and round, gathering momentum, breathing steadily. In through the nose. Out through the mouth. In through the nose. Out through the mouth.

Bang! Bang! Bang! Bang! on the walls. His arm aching, the shaft whirling in front of his eyes. Slightly dizzy now.

Then he felt the gears mesh and he was in the zone.

"Now!" he yelled.

The Prince stooped, forming a stirrup with his hands. Zak flung himself hard at the back wall and rebounded, one foot lifting into Viktor's hands.

He surged upwards, boosted by the Prince.

The gate was too far away.

Impossible to reach.

Then it wasn't. It was easy.

His fingers caught on the metal threshold of the doorway. He heard the Prince shout something encouraging. He hung at full stretch for a few moments, then pulled with all his might. He got an elbow under the gate. He swung his leg up, getting a foothold.

Straining every muscle in his body, he heaved himself up so that he was standing pressed against the gate with his toes on the threshold and his arms wrapped around the criss-crossing steel strips.

He looked down and saw Viktor's pale face staring at him.

"Piece of cake," he gasped under his breath.

He edged to one side and eased the gate open, slowly so as not to trap his fingers as the mesh of steel rods scissored together.

He gestured to the Prince, putting a finger to his lips to indicate silence. He didn't know where Max and Bruno were. Until he was sure they had gone, they had to keep quiet.

He jogged across the floor. The truck was still there. That wasn't good. Were the two men still in the building?

He found a length of rope curled among some rubbish. He ran back to the lift shaft and fed it down, tying the end to the gate. The Prince pulled himself up.

"Wait until I tell Father about this," gasped Viktor. "You'll get a medal for sure."

"That's great," said Zak. "But we need to get out of here first. Follow me."

The main gates to the warehouse were locked. No chance of escape the easy way, then. They made their way to the staircase. The swing doors led to a corridor with doors leading off on either side.

They ran along the corridor. This time Zak was careful to keep Viktor close by his side, even though his muscles ached to be let loose. It was hard, running at normal speed when every fibre of his body was crying out to go faster.

Zak tried a few doors, but the rooms were empty except for rubbish, and the windows were sealed. This place hadn't been used for some time. There was a window at the far end of the corridor. The bottom pane was smashed. The window looked out over a huge scrapyard filled with scrap metal and the piled hulks of cars.

There was a chunk of brick lying in a scattering of glass shards on the floor. Someone had lobbed the brick to break the window. For fun, Zak assumed.

He picked up the piece of brick and used it to chip away the remaining glass fragments from around the lower frame. Once the spikes of broken glass were gone, the hole would be big enough for them to get through.

He winced at the noise, but there was no way to do it quietly.

It didn't take long.

"You first," he told Viktor. The Prince folded himself up and squeezed through the gap. He perched on the sill for a moment then jumped the two-metre drop into the yard.

Excellent! Finally a plan had worked. Now all he had to do . . .

A small popping sound interrupted his thoughts.

Almost instantaneously the pane of glass above his head shattered, spilling jagged shards down over him. He snapped his head around.

Max was running towards him along the corridor, and Bruno was right behind. The soft pop had been a bullet from the silenced gun.

Zak was head first through the window frame in a moment. He crashed into the side of a car wreck, landing in a heap on the ground. But he was up again, almost quicker than thought.

"Run!" he yelled.

He snatched hold of Viktor's arm as they zigzagged through the piles of rusty metal. A shot whined as it ricocheted off a hulk of old steel. Zak glanced back in time to see the two men jumping down.

High piles of scrap metal and wrecked car bodies formed narrow aisles that wound like a maze through the scrapyard. Zak ran, jinking nimbly at sudden corners, never slowing down, dragging the Prince along with him.

He could hear the pounding of pursuing feet.

He glanced at Viktor. The Prince's face was running with sweat and he was holding his side. Zak knew Viktor needed a breather. He turned suddenly and dived into a narrow gap between two cars, hauling the panting Prince in after him. There was a small space for them to hide in.

"Get your breath back," he whispered.

Viktor gulped in air. "I'll be . . . fine . . . in a moment . . ." he panted. "It's a . . . stitch, that's all. We need to . . . find people . . ." He paused, taking a deep breath. "They won't follow us . . . where there are people . . ."

Zak looked at the Prince thoughtfully. True, that had been his initial plan as well – to escape from the two men and get the Prince to safety. But something Colonel Hunter had once said kept banging away in his head.

Ordinary people run away from trouble – Project 17 agents run towards it. He couldn't just run away – he wasn't ordinary people any more. He had to do something to take those two thugs down.

He looked at Viktor. "I've got an idea," he said. "I could try it on my own, but I'm not going to risk them finding you, so we have to do it together. Are you up for that?"

"What idea?"

"We dive deep," Zak said.

The Prince frowned. "What does that mean?"

"It means we need to try and find a manhole," said Zak. "Wait here, I'm going to take a look around."

He began to climb, making his way cautiously up through the stack of mangled cars. It wasn't easy – there were a lot of rusty edges that gave way under his feet, and the pile wasn't as stable as he would have liked. On the way, he looked around, searching for something he would need. There! That would do the trick. He reached out and grabbed a small twisted length of steel, shoving it into the front of his shirt for later.

He came to the top and perched for a few moments, taking the time to get a clear 360-degree view of their surroundings.

"Got it!" he said under his breath. A railway viaduct ran along one side of the scrapyard. Not too far to run.

He climbed back down again. Time to put his plan into action.

A four-metre high chain-link fence barred the way to the deserted road running alongside the railway viaduct. Zak and the Prince reached it without encountering the two men.

Zak jogged along the fence, looking for a gap or split. He found a place where the fence had been pulled away from one of the metal posts. Easy to squeeze underneath. He lifted the chain-link and Victor crawled through. Then he let it drop again.

Victor stood on the other side. Puzzled.

"What are you waiting for?" he asked. "I'll hold the fence up for you."

"I'm going to climb up over the top," Zak told him.

"That's crazy. They'll see you."

Zak nodded. "I want them to." He pointed through the fence. "See that?" Viktor turned, staring towards a large square inspection hatch set into the road. "We're going down there – and I want those two meatheads to follow us."

Understanding lit up in Viktor's eyes. "We're going to lure them down and trap them?" he said. "Can we really do that?"

"We have to try," Zak said. "If we can capture them, my boss will make them talk and we'll know what MARS are planning. We'll be able to stop them hurting your parents."

"But what about the gun?" asked Viktor.

Zak grimaced. "That's the tricky part," he said. "Go and wait by the manhole. I won't be long."

He grabbed the fence and began to climb while Viktor ran across to the inspection hatch. The fence was rickety and loose, but Zak got to the top without any problems. He looked back across the scrapyard. This was going to be dicey. He wanted to be seen, but he very much didn't want to get shot. He'd have to time this to perfection.

He hooked a leg over the top of the fence, then jerked back and forth, making the fence rattle. He glimpsed a movement among the piles of cars. A bald head, shining for a moment in the sunlight. Max?

Rattle, rattle, rattle.

One of the men appeared. Bruno. He saw Zak and shouted.

That was it. Job done!

Zak turned awkwardly, clinging to the fence, judging the fall – then he jumped. He landed with knees bent to absorb the impact. He raced to where Viktor was waiting. He pulled the bent length of steel from his shirt.

"Did they see you?" Viktor asked.

Zak nodded. He pushed the bent end of the steel rod into the keyhole of the hatch and heaved upwards. "Help me!" he gasped. "It's heavy."

Working together the two of them strained to lift the heavy inspection hatch. It rose, tilted on its end and fell backwards with a resounding clang.

"There'll be a metal ladder bolted to the wall," Zak said. "You go first." He felt in his pocket and pushed the pencil torch into the Prince's hand. "Take this. It'll be dark."

He waited while Viktor clambered into the hole. The powerful beam of the torch lit up the grime and filth at the bottom of the shaft. Zak really hoped this was going to work.

He flashed a glance towards the fence. The two men were almost there. Max came crashing into the fence, aiming his gun through the mesh.

Zak had no more time. "I'm coming down!" he shouted as he stepped off and dropped feet first into the shaft, moments before a bullet whined above his head, close enough almost to part his hair.

This had better work; otherwise he'd just led Prince Viktor into mortal danger.

CHAPTER **THIRTEEN**

The narrow tunnel was low and damp and it smelled bad. Thick cables were stapled to the walls, hanging in heavy loops, dangling filthy cobwebs. Thin white roots hung from the curved brickwork ceiling and there was the constant sound of dripping water.

"What is this?" hissed Viktor. "Where are we?"

They had been underground for a few minutes now, moving quickly but cautiously. It was slimy and treacherous underfoot. Zak flashed the white beam down the long stretch of the tunnel. "I don't know," he whispered back.

"But I thought . . ."

"I mean I don't know *yet*," murmured Zak. "I'm looking for something. When I find it, I'll be able to . . . a-ha!" Something on the wall ahead reflected the light back. Zak ran towards it. It was a small metal plaque. Some letters and numbers were stamped into it.

PS7485X

Zak stood staring at the code-mark, wracking his brains to try and remember what it meant. He closed his eyes, picturing in his mind the map that Colonel Hunter had given him of all the tunnels and passages and walkways that ran under London. He'd studied that map for hours, priding himself on remembering every detail. How every sewer pipe and disused underground train tunnel fitted together, how every electrical cable channel and wartime rat run were linked under the streets.

"This is good," he murmured at last. "I think this leads in the right direction." He stared back along the way they had come. The utility tunnel had taken a few sharp bends and it had split off in various directions. Had the two thugs followed them down here or had they given up?

Zak was sure he'd heard echoing footsteps behind them at first. But if the thugs had no way of lighting the tunnel, they might have turned back.

He thought he heard a scuffling sound back there. He

switched off the torch, listening intently. A light bobbed at the far end, yellowish and not as strong as his own beam, but definitely torchlight.

Bruno and Max were still on the case.

He switched the torch back on and nudged the Prince to follow. A foggy, booming voice echoed down the tunnel. No words, just an angry noise, along with rapid footfalls that reverberated like distant thunder. Max and Bruno had seen the torchlight. They were coming fast and they were not happy.

The tunnel divided again. There was an arched exit leading to a much bigger shaft that plunged down many metres. A metal ladder was stapled to the wall, circled with hoops of steel. Zak played the torch beam over the metal plaque at the top of the shaft. TX023.

Yes. He knew that code. They were heading in the right direction.

He gestured with the torch. "Down," he said. "You go first. I'll light the way."

He hovered at the top of the ladder, shining the light as the Prince descended. The sound of running feet was getting louder and he could see the yellowy light again.

He waited until the last moment, then turned and began to descend, as fast as he could, hand over hand, the slim torch held between his teeth.

Viktor was waiting for him at the bottom of the shaft. They had come to a larger tunnel now – a semicircle of old brickwork that stretched away in either direction. Heavy-jointed metal pipes ran along the curved walls and the floor was of close-fitting black bricks.

Zak ran his torch over the walls. Where was it?

The metal plaque glinted. CT9687B.

Oh, yes! That was very good.

Their heads jerked up at a noise from above. Their pursuers were at the top of the ladder. Time to go!

They put on speed now. Not *zone* speed, but enough to give them a good start.

The tunnel wound off in a long smooth curve. Zak glanced over his shoulder, seeing the dim yellowy light bobbing on the walls behind.

Viktor let out a cry of alarm.

The tunnel ended abruptly in a solid brick wall. There were no doors – no forks. Nothing.

Alarm shot through Zak as he jogged to a halt, staring at the wall. What if he had remembered it wrong? Rats in a trap.

"Now what?" gasped Viktor.

Zak roved the torch beam over the wall.

There had to be something.

Then he saw a small grey metal box, clamped to the

bottom of the side of the tunnel. He dropped to his knees, fumbling at the screw catch that held the box closed.

The tunnel was filled with the thudding of running feet.

Zak pulled the front of the box away. There was a small keypad inside. He tapped in his personal code. QSP17.

He stood up, his heart beating hard. There was a deep grinding sound as the blocking wall began slowly to move sideways.

A white light flooded out from beyond the sliding wall.

Zak caught hold of Viktor's arm and dragged him through into a brightly lit tunnel with smooth white walls. Fluorescent tubing ran along the arched ceiling. A red light was strobing.

Zak stayed absolutely still, facing the way they had come, holding onto Viktor's arm as the brick wall slid away. Bruno and Max approached slowly, blinking in the sudden fierce light. Max raised his gun, aiming it at Zak.

"You don't want to do that," Zak called. "You want to put that nasty thing down and surrender."

Max said something in his own language, striding forwards now, the gun held level at the height of Zak's forehead. Bruno caught his arm, blinking and shielding his eyes, saying something that sounded like a warning.

Running feet came behind Zak. He didn't even bother to look around as the black-clad men moved forwards with their automatic weapons at the ready. Max's gun clattered to the floor. Both men lifted their hands. Zak loved the look of shock and awe that appeared on their ugly mugs.

He smiled. "Welcome to Citadel, guys," he said. "I think the word I'm looking for is . . . *gotcha*!"

Citadel, Bastion, Rampart, Fortress. The four secret British Intelligence complexes deep under London. Each run by a separate department, and each with its own mission statement and purpose, but all of them linked, all of them working for the security of the United Kingdom and the safety and protection of its citizens.

A private underground railway whisked Zak and Prince Viktor through the tunnel that led north from Citadel to Fortress. On arrival in Colonel Hunter's domain, Bruno and Max were handed over to Project 17 agents while Zak and Viktor were taken to a comfortable room where food and drink were provided to help them recover from their ordeal.

Viktor was wired, teeming with questions, and it was hard for Zak to avoid giving him the answers he craved. Where exactly were they? How big was this place? How many people worked here? Who knew about it?

"We're under London . . . it's pretty big . . . oh, quite a few . . . uh, well, not all that many . . ."

Vague, unhelpful answers. But Zak had no idea what he was allowed to tell the Prince. The existence of Fortress was classified as Top Secret. You couldn't get more secret than that.

Zak was relieved when Colonel Hunter entered. He handed Viktor a Mob. "You'll want to take this call, Your Highness," he said. "It's your father."

While Viktor talked excitedly to the King, Colonel Hunter led Zak out into the corridor. "I'm going to have the Prince taken to his parents under close escort," he told Zak. "I want you to sit in on the interrogation of the two kidnappers. You might have some useful insights."

"I know they work for Alfonso Gecko," said Zak. "Are they part of MARS?"

"That's one of the things we need to find out," said the Colonel. He took a Mob from his jacket pocket. "This is to replace your old one," he said, handing it to Zak. "Bug has programmed everything into it." He paused, looking at him hard. Zak wondered for a moment whether he was about to get a word or two of praise. A job well done. The Prince saved. Not that he expected it. But, still . . .

"When this is all over," the Colonel said quietly, "you and I need to have a conversation about your misuse of Bug's time and Project 17's resources." He turned and strode down the corridor, leaving Zak standing in his wake with a cold feeling in his stomach. "Come on," the Colonel said, turning back to face him. "You need to focus. The King is determined to make his speech at the conference in just over an hour, so we don't have much time."

Zak caught up with the Colonel, struggling to keep his mind on the problem in hand.

There was no time for him to worry about Hunter's ominous words – the danger to the Royal Family wasn't over yet.

It was a small, bleak grey room, lit to eye-watering brightness. A plain metal-topped table stood in the middle of the cement floor, with two chairs on one side and two on the other. A large mirror filled one wall. Cameras pointed down from two corners of the ceiling. A black recording device stood on a side table, the LED lights on its display screen rising and falling as the Colonel asked his questions.

Zak sat next to Colonel Hunter, staring across the table at Bruno and Max. They looked as brutal and unpleasant as ever, but the fact that they were both handcuffed made them seem a lot less dangerous.

The Colonel had an open folder in front of him, and as he asked the questions, he made brief notes of the answers. Max was sullen and closed-mouthed. Bruno was doing most of the talking, although he wasn't exactly being helpful.

The Colonel flicked through some documents. "Bruno Szabo," he said, without looking up. "A Hungarian ex-pat wanted by the police of seven European states." He turned over a page. "Max Varga. Also Hungarian. Drug smuggler, hitman." The Colonel's eyebrows rose a little. "Wanted in *nine* European states."

Now he looked across at the two men. "Who sent you to London, and what is your mission here?"

"We demand to see a representative from the Hungarian Embassy," said Bruno, glowering at the Colonel. "We say nothing."

"Were you sent by Alfonso Gecko?" the Colonel asked.

"I never heard of the man," said Bruno.

"That's a lie," said Zak. "I saw you with him."

Bruno glared at him. "Who is this child?" he asked. "Why is he here?"

"I saw you on the *Goodfellow*," Zak said coolly, holding Bruno's evil stare. "Your pal was playing cards and you were reading a magazine."

"What nonsense is this?" Bruno snarled, and the look in Max's eyes was murderous. "The boy is crazy. Send him away."

"Remember Mr Gecko sent you out after you heard a noise?" Zak reminded him. "Just after Rafe left? That noise was me."

Max bared his teeth as though he would like to bite chunks out of Zak.

"We know of your connection to Mr Gecko," said Colonel Hunter. "What I want from you now is his connection to MARS."

Zak got the impression that the two thugs were taken aback.

"We know nothing of this," shouted Bruno. "Who tells these lies about us?"

"MARS are planning an attack on the King while he's in London," Colonel Hunter said, his voice perfectly calm. "We believe the kidnapping of Prince Viktor was part of this attack. I need you to tell me what else MARS is intending to do. If you cooperate with us, it may be possible to work out a deal. If you don't, you'll be handed over to the appropriate authorities in Hungary or Germany or Italy or any one of several other countries, where you will doubtless spend the rest of your lives behind bars."

There was a long silence while the two men took this in. Bruno hissed something to Max – in Hungarian, Zak assumed. Max spat something back.

Bruno shook his head, looking now at the Colonel. "We know nothing of MARS," he said. "We are not terrorists. We work for Mr Gecko. We do business for him. He tells us, go to London and kidnap the boy from the hotel. He gives us our instructions. The number of the hotel room. A safe place to keep the Prince till the ransom is paid." He sneered. "It is nothing to do with MARS. It is a private matter between Mr Gecko and the Prince. It is purely a business arrangement."

"You will need to explain that," said the Colonel. "What was the private matter between Prince Viktor and Mr. Gecko?"

"No, not the boy," Bruno retorted. "The other Prince."

"You mean Rafe?" Zak broke in.

"Yes, Rafe," said Bruno. "He owes Mr Gecko a great deal of money, so Mr Gecko says, give me my money or you will suffer. The boy blubs a little and begs for time. Mr Gecko is a reasonable man. He gives the boy three days, and he says, get the money from your uncle – he is rich. But the boy says King Edgar will not give him money. Mr Gecko says, he will give you money to save his son's life."

"So the kidnapping was organized to raise funds to pay back Prince Rafe's debts to Mr Gecko?" said the Colonel. "Is that what you're telling me?"

"Sure," said Bruno. "It's business, you know? We would never have hurt the boy."

"Your pal shot at me," Zak exclaimed.

Bruno shrugged. "You, we didn't care about so much," he said. "You were not worth any money to us."

"Oh, thanks," said Zak. A sudden thought hit him. "I heard you talking on the phone in that warehouse," he said. "You wanted to change the deal – you wanted more money. You were talking to Rafe, weren't you? You were double crossing him."

"It was business," said Bruno. "The boy is a weak fool. We thought we could get more money. Why not?"

There was another silence. At last, Colonel Hunter spoke. "I'm not convinced," he said. "Your boss has been linked to MARS. I need you to tell me what has been planned. I need details of when and where the attack is to take place, and I need to know the nature of the attack."

A soft croaking sounded from Zak's pocket. Bug – on the new Mob. Zak put it to his ear.

"Tell Control I've located the source of the ransom email," Bug said.

Zak relayed the message to Colonel Hunter.

"Find Switchblade and Wildcat," said the Colonel. "Check it out. I've got more work to do here."

Zak slipped out of the interview room and ran to Bug's office. On the way he texted Switch and Cat to tell them what was happening.

"It was tricky," Bug said as Zak leaned over the back of his chair and stared at the plasma screen. It showed a satellite image of London. "I had to chase him all over the planet, but the source turned out to be right . . ." He tapped the keyboard and the image zoomed in on the centre of the city. ". . . About . . . " The image blew up even more, showing streets and grey buildings coming closer and closer. ". . . Here!" Bug smiled. "I've pinned him down to within ten centimetres."

It took Zak about three seconds to recognize the aerial view.

"Trafalgar Square!" he gasped.

"Bingo!" said Bug. "And whoever sent the email is still there." He grinned. "He's probably feeding the pigeons." He looked up at Zak. "I'd go and get him if I were you," he said. "Before he gets bored and wanders off."

"You bet!" Three seconds later, Zak was running along another Fortress corridor, heading for a lift to ground level, speed-dialling Switchblade with the news.

Prince Rafe was sitting on the stone edge of the fountain in the middle of Trafalgar Square when Zak and Switch and Wildcat walked up to him through the crowds of tourists.

He had a laptop on his knees.

He seemed more relieved than surprised as the three agents appeared in front of him. He looked up at them, and his eyes were desperate.

"*Est-il sûr?*" he blurted. "Is Viktor all right?"

"Yes, he is," said Switchblade. "Thanks to Quicksilver."

"And no thanks to you," added Cat. "How could you do it?"

"I was desperate," said the Prince sadly. "Desperate people do desperate things."

"Give me the laptop and come with us," said Switch. "You've got some explaining to do."

*

Zak was sitting in a small viewing cubicle behind the two-way mirror in Interrogation Room P05 in Fortress. Through the glass he could see a room very similar to the one he had been in earlier with the Colonel and the two thugs. Except now it was Prince Rafe on the wrong side of the metal table, and Switchblade and Wildcat doing the interrogating.

Their voices came clearly through a loudspeaker.

"I got deeper and deeper into debt," Rafe was saying. "And when Gecko suggested the idea of a fake kidnapping, it seemed to be my only chance."

"*Fake* kidnapping?" commented Wildcat. "They had a gun – they were threatening to send your cousin back in bite-sized pieces. How is that *fake*?"

"That was not part of the deal," said Rafe. "They should not have behaved like that."

"But *you* sent the ransom email," said Switch. "Demanding five million pounds and threatening to do grievous bodily harm to Prince Viktor if the money wasn't handed over."

"They told me to do it. What else could I have done?" cried Rafe. "I was helpless." He dropped his head into his hands. "I never wanted to come to London," he groaned. "Uncle Edgar should not have let Jorum persuade him to bring me here. If I had remained in Montevisto, I would have been spared *tout ce mal*! All this trouble!"

Zak felt like giving him a swift kick up the rear. Rafe had created chaos and alarm, and all he could think about was himself.

"You could have refused to come," said Switchblade.

"Jorum was adamant that we *all* come on the trip," said Rafe, lifting his face again. "He said it would be the perfect photo opportunity when the whole Royal Family were together at the world premiere of that new dinosaur computer game." He snorted. "As if I would be interested in such *absurdité*! Such nonsense!"

Zak's Mob chimed. Hunter's ringtone. Zak picked it up to find a brief text message.

"MI5 says King's speech has gone off without a hitch. King, Queen and Chancellor now being driven to Natural History Museum to meet Prince V. Nothing suspicious. All looking good."

Rafe's voice brought Zak's attention back to the interrogation.

"That is absurd! I have nothing to do with those terrorists! *Êtes-vous foux?* Are you insane? They killed my mother and father. I hate them!"

Obviously Switch or Cat had asked him if he knew about the MARS death threats. Apparently not, if the expression on his face was anything to go by. He looked genuinely horrified by the idea.

Switch wasn't about to be put off by Rafe's denials. "So the phrase '*When The Tyrant King Speaks, His Roar Will Bring Death To The House Of Corvetti*' doesn't mean anything to you?" he asked.

"Nothing at all!" insisted the Prince. "My uncle is no tyrant! No sane person would call him that!"

Zak frowned. *When The Tyrant King Speaks.* Distant bells were ringing in his head now. Alarm bells. Getting louder all the time.

The Tyrant King.

Did that mean something else, perhaps? Nothing to do with King Edgar?

He got up and ran for the door. Thirty seconds later he was in Bug's office.

"Can you access the promo video for the TR3000?" he asked. "Quickly!"

Bug recognized the urgency in his voice. He tapped his keyboard and a video appeared on-screen. The same one Viktor had shown Zak in his Mesozoic Madhouse in the Palace.

But this time, it wasn't the people playing the game in the foreground that Zak was looking at. This time he was staring at what was going on behind them.

Animatronic dinosaurs.

Moving, life-like dinosaurs.

One of them was a T-rex.

"The 'T' in T-rex stands for *tyrannosaurus*, doesn't it?" Zak said.

"That's right," said Bug, looking around at Zak. "The full name is Tyrannosaurus rex. So what?"

"That's not English, is it?" Zak said, the urgency growing in his voice. "What does it *mean*?"

"I think it's Latin or Ancient Greek, or something like that," said Bug as his fingers flew over the keys. "Yes – here we are. Tyrannosaurus rex – from the Greek, meaning . . . ohh . . . it means . . ." His voice trailed off as he stared at the wide plasma screen.

"Tyrant King," breathed Zak. "*Tyrant King!*" He spun round, already running. "I have to tell the Colonel," he called back as he raced along the corridor. "We've had it wrong from the very beginning! Something bad is going to happen at the Natural History Museum – at the premiere of the TR3000 – and the Royal Family is going to be right in the middle of it!"

CHAPTER **FOURTEEN**

Two black transit vans came to a screaming halt outside the front gates of the Natural History Museum. Tourists scattered as black-clad agents spilled out and raced across the courtyard towards the imposing twin towers that reared above the great arched entranceway.

As fast as they moved, one figure outstripped them all, taking the stone steps four at a time, cutting through the alarmed bystanders and sprinting into the foyer of the museum at an incredible speed.

Zak was so in the zone that he had hardly been able to contain himself in the back of the van. He felt as if he wanted to jump clean out of his skin, as if his muscles were revved to breaking point. As if he was about to explode.

Colonel Hunter had called ahead, alerting the MI5 protection teams that there was potential danger in the museum. The whole place was closed to the general public for the afternoon, but there were plenty of specially invited guests: VIPS, Government officials, employees of the company that had created the TR3000 game, a bunch of influential bloggers and reviewers, not to mention a massive gaggle of media people, all desperate for a look at the Montevisto Royal Family and all wanting to be the first to report on this major new breakthrough in computer game technology.

Ushers and officials were already herding the VIP guests out of the Dinosaur Gallery and across the cathedral-like expanse of the central hall with its gothic arches and sculptures.

The massive black skeleton of a Diplodocus towered up, dominating the floor space. The hurrying people surged around it like floodwater, their faces anxious as they jostled to get out. Zak pushed against the human tide. There was some barging and shouting, but so far the exodus was reasonably orderly and civilized. So far.

Zak fought his way to the left – towards the Dinosaur

Gallery – slowed by the crowd, struggling onwards, desperate to get through.

The entrance was clogged with film crews and TV reporters, and with people carrying shoulder-mounted video cameras and unwieldy boom microphones.

An amplified voice rang out clearly from within.

"Please move calmly to the exits. The museum needs to be evacuated. Please do not panic. There is no cause for alarm. This is a purely precautionary measure." The voice began to get a little more insistent. "The camera crews and photographers in the doorways need to get out – *now*!"

Zak ducked down to avoid getting sideswiped by a whirling boom mike as the clog of people began to surge into the central hall. He dived in among them, fighting his way into the Gallery.

Finally he was in!

He didn't have time to look at his surroundings. He was vaguely aware of large colourful wall murals of prehistoric forests, and of wall-mounted screens with graphics of some kind of underwater battle between thrashing monsters. Animatronic dinosaurs lifted their heads from Jurassic set-piece scenes, their eyes gleaming and their jaws opening and closing while growls, snarls and roars echoed through the Gallery.

The Royal Family was standing together behind a semicircle of MI5 agents in dark suits. The agents were facing outwards, holding their guns two-handed. Ready for any attack.

King Edgar stood with his arm protectively around the Queen's shoulders, his face composed and unafraid. Viktor was in front of them, his solemn eyes darting this way and that, anxious but not panicky. From the corner of his eye, Zak saw something that didn't seem particularly significant. Chancellor Jorum among the camera crews and photographers, heading for the way out.

But Zak's attention was focused on something else. Something right behind the Royals. Something that really had him worried.

An animatronic T-rex.

He shoved his way towards the ring of armed agents.

The T-rex lifted its great wedge-shaped head and its tooth-filled mouth opened. A very realistic roar reverberated through the gallery.

When The Tyrant King Speaks, His Roar Will Bring Death To The House Of Corvetti.

Zak ran forwards. "Get them away from the T-rex!" he yelled. The seven agents reacted immediately, swinging their automatic pistols around and aiming them directly at his chest.

Alarmed, he came to a skidding halt.

"Step back," one of them barked. "We're authorized to use deadly force!"

"I'm on your side," shouted Zak. "Codename Quicksilver. Project 17. You have to listen to me – you have to . . ."

"Move back!" the voice cracked like gunfire. "You won't be warned again."

They didn't believe him. If he took another step they'd probably shoot.

The T-rex's head turned and Zak had the weird feeling that it was looking at him as it opened its mouth again.

"Code Winter!" Zak yelled. "Get them out of here! *Code Winter!* Get them out *now*!"

The reaction of the MI5 agents to the codeword was instantaneous. One of them snapped, "Platinum protocol. Delta formation!" The agents formed a tight ring around the three Royals and rushed them towards the exit.

Zak saw a startled look on the King's face as he was hustled away with his arm still around the Queen's shoulders. Viktor was there too, but Zak couldn't see him above the tightly packed bodies of the MI5 agents as they barged their way out through the doorway.

Zak let out a gasp of relief.

The T-rex's roar echoed along the Gallery.

He began to turn away.

A white flash blinded him and the roar of the dinosaur was drowned out by a massive explosion.

The world blazed red and black.

A wave of intense heat lifted Zak off his feet and threw him the length of the gallery.

He slithered along the floor, his arms up to protect his head. He came to a halt against the far wall, gasping for breath. Debris rained down on him, broken glass and splinters of wood and chunks of twisted metal. Something big and heavy crashed down a few millimetres from where he lay.

The noise died down and he opened his eyes.

The charred and blackened head of the T-rex stared at him with one cracked and glittering eye.

He scrabbled away from it, heart hammering.

Thick dark smoke was billowing around him and his ears were ringing from the detonation. Keeping low, he slithered along the floor towards the exit, trying not to breathe in the toxic fumes.

Shrill alarms were howling. He saw a shaft of light through the smoke.

The exit!

As he crawled closer, he saw the shaft shrinking from

the top down. An automatic fire door was descending.

"No! Wait!"

He flung himself forwards and rolled under the falling metal door. It scraped his shoulder as he came spinning out into the hallway.

He scrambled to his feet, dizzy and with his head full of noise. Mission accomplished. He had saved the Royals.

Way to go, Agent Quicksilver!

The scene that confronted him was so unexpected that for a moment he didn't believe his eyes.

The Chancellor was up against a wall, one arm crooked around Viktor's neck, his other hand holding a gun to the Prince's temple. There was a look of almost animal anger and hatred on his face.

The MI5 agents were facing him, guns raised, blocking his way forwards.

"Do not shoot!" shouted the King. "Johannes? Why are you doing this?"

"You old fool!" snarled the Chancellor, tightening his grip around the Prince's neck so that Viktor winced in pain. "You should have abdicated when you had the chance!"

The Queen lunged forwards, her arms reaching for her son. An agent caught hold of her, pulling her back. "How could you do this to us?" she called to the Chancellor. "We trusted you."

"MARS should govern Montevisto," snarled Jorum. "The monarchy should be extinct." His voice rose to a cracked shout. "Stand back. I am leaving now – the Prince will die if anyone attempts to stop me."

"Do as he says," said the MI5 leader. "Stand down, everyone."

Jorum moved along the wall, dragging Viktor with him, the gun unwavering at the side of the Prince's head. The MI5 agents lowered their guns as the Chancellor made for a side entrance.

Zak's eyes met Viktor's.

Stay cool! Zak projected the thought. *I'll get you out of this.*

Not that he had any idea how he might do that. But he'd grown to like the Prince. Rescuing him wasn't just a duty any more – this was about friendship too.

The Chancellor and his hostage were at the exit now.

"If anyone follows, the Prince dies!" Jorum shouted. The door slid open and he backed through it.

Zak turned and raced into the central hall. Virtually all the guests were gone now. Switchblade, Cat and the other Project 17 agents were there, running to join the MI5 teams.

Switch caught Zak's arm. "Jorum?" he said. "Jorum all along?"

Zak nodded. "I have to go," he said, pulling free of Switchblade's grip.

"Wait! Where?"

But Zak didn't have time to explain.

He sprinted to the main entrance, elbowing past the few remaining people, avoiding the TV crews reporting live on the steps.

In the zone.

He leaped over the curved stone parapet of the steps, coming down onto clipped grass. He ran along the front of the museum, passing tall trees as he reached the edge of the building. He jerked back out of sight. Jorum was running across an oval courtyard, dragging Viktor with him. He was heading towards a path that led under more trees to a wrought-iron gate and the open road beyond.

Zak kept under the cover of the trees, as he moved in to head the Chancellor off.

There was still the problem of the gun. Even at top speed, could he take the Chancellor down before he put a bullet in Viktor's head? Did he even dare try?

He darted through the trees. He could see the Chancellor, moving fast for a guy of his age, pulling

Viktor with him despite the Prince's struggles to break free.

Jorum came to the gate and burst out onto the pavement. Looping his arm around Viktor's neck, Jorum swung his gun at the passing pedestrians. They scattered in panic.

Jorum dragged the Prince to the curb. Heavy traffic filled the wide road, two lanes deep in either direction. As Zak slid from cover and approached the gate, the cars and vans and buses came to a stop. At the junction of Queensgate Mews and Cromwell Road, the traffic lights had changed to red.

Jorum moved to a car caught in the line of stalled traffic, holding the gun at arm's length, pointing it at the terrified driver.

"Get out!" he shouted.

The driver threw the door open and scrambled out, cringing as he fled. Jorum bundled Viktor into the car and pushed in after him, slamming the door.

Crazy! The car was blocked by bumper-to-bumper traffic. Where did Jorum think he could go?

Zak didn't have to wait long to find out.

Wrenching at the wheel, the Chancellor revved the motor. The car gave a lurch, smashing into the back of the car in front, sending it jerking forwards. The Chancellor's face was filled with controlled fury as he backed the car up, twisting the wheel and gunning the motor. The car surged forwards again, turning sharply and bumping up over the curb.

There were screams and shouts of fear from pedestrians as the car mounted the pavement and hurtled alongside the line of standing traffic.

Zak staggered back as the car grazed past him, gathering speed.

He stared after it for a split second before his instincts kicked in.

Then he ran after the car.

It accelerated, drawing away from him. Fixing his eyes on the rear window, Zak moved up a gear or two, his legs pumping, his feet eating up the gap. In the zone.

He was close to the back bumper now. He threw himself forwards, snatching for a handhold as his feet left the ground.

His fingers closed around the short aerial that jutted from the back of the car's roof. His body slammed against the sloping hatchback window.

He scrabbled with his feet, trying to get some kind of purchase on the back of the car. His toes pressed on a solid edge and he boosted himself up onto the roof.

The car slewed from side to side as Zak clung on.

Jorum was trying to throw him off. But he gritted his teeth, spreadeagled on the car's slippery roof, refusing to let go.

Kicking against the aerial, Zak slid forwards. He twisted around and came legs first off the front of the roof, sliding across the windscreen, his body blocking the Chancellor's line of sight.

Zak jammed his toes against the windscreen wipers, folding his legs and looking in at the Chancellor, wondering whether he should try and kick the windscreen in. A desperate sight met his eyes. Viktor had hold of Jorum's gun hand and the two of them were struggling furiously.

The steering wheel spun.

The car lurched to the side and ploughed along the railings. Metal screamed against metal, spitting sparks. There was a loud bang as the car hit a stone pillar. The front crumpled and Zak found himself tumbling through the air. Tucking his head in, he rolled unhurt across the pavement. He leaped up and ran back to the car.

He dragged the passenger door open and yanked Viktor out.

"Are you okay?" he gasped.

The Prince nodded dazedly. Chancellor Jorum was slumped to one side, his head lolling, a thin trail of blood running from his hairline.

Zak crawled in, switching the engine off and retrieving the gun from between the Chancellor's feet.

Viktor looked at him with shining eyes. "That was so cool!" he said.

A sudden weakness hit Zak behind the knees and he dropped to sit on the pavement, aware that he hurt all over. "Thanks," he said, flooded with relief as he realized that the mission was finally at an end. "It was nothing." He smiled up at the Prince. "All in a day's work."

CHAPTER **FIFTEEN**

06.00. FORTRESS.
THE FOLLOWING MORNING.

Zak sat with other Project 17 agents as Colonel Hunter presented the mission report. He felt weary and battered, but despite that he was in good spirits. He'd messed up a few times, but in the end, he'd come good. He'd brought the Chancellor down single-handedly.

"Johannes Jorum has been charged with attempted murder and offences under the Explosive Substances Act," the Colonel reported. "As his offences occurred on UK soil, he will be tried here."

"Was he the boss of MARS?" asked Wildcat.

"He was," said the Colonel. "He set up and ran the whole organization from the start. His hope at first was to force the King to abdicate and declare a republic – a republic with Mr Jorum as its President. When that failed, he decided the Corvetti family had to die."

It made a kind of twisted sense, Zak thought. That was why Jorum had insisted Rafe should come to London – so he could get all four of the Royals together in one place to blow them up, using one of the MARS sleeper cells he had already set up here. What he hadn't planned on was that Rafe would do a deal with Alfonso Gecko to kidnap Prince Viktor to pay off his gambling debts.

Without meaning to, Rafe had probably saved all their lives. It was when Rafe had said, "My uncle is no tyrant!" that Zak had started wondering about the real meaning of the words "the Tyrant King".

"Prince Rafe has been flown back to Montevisto under escort," Colonel Hunter said, his report echoing Zak's thoughts. "He will be a key witness in the trial of Alfonso Gecko."

"I wonder if Rafe has learned his lesson," murmured Switchblade.

"I saw him before he was taken away," said the Colonel.

"He was genuinely shaken by what almost happened to Prince Viktor. The King believes the shock of recent events will bring him to his senses, and I'm sure he's right."

Let's hope so, thought Zak.

"On to other news," the Colonel continued. "The MARS cell responsible for planting the bomb has been picked up. Bruno Szabo and Max Varga have been handed over to the Metropolitan Police and have been charged with kidnapping. They've already made a deal to tell Interpol everything they know about Alfonso Gecko's criminal empire in exchange for lighter sentences." He referred to his notes. "The Royals are due to depart from Heathrow within the next few hours." He frowned a little. "I have been asked by King Edgar to convey his deepest gratitude to those agents involved in this mission. He also asked that I grant Agents Switchblade, Wildcat and Quicksilver a few days' leave to fly to Montevisto for a brief holiday at the King's expense."

Zak's ears perked up. A holiday in the Med. Way to go, King Edgar!

"I explained to the King that such a reward was both inappropriate and unnecessary," the Colonel continued.

Zak's shoulders slumped.

"But he told me that the Crown Prince insisted, so I have decided to comply with his request," the Colonel added. "Following the explosion at the Natural History Museum, the premiere of the TR3000 computer game will now be taking place in Montevisto." He looked at the three agents. "Switchblade, Wildcat, Quicksilver, you are granted a seventy-two-hour leave. This will allow you to attend the premiere. A car will be waiting to take you to Heathrow Airport at zero eight hundred hours." He snapped the file closed. "That's all. Dismissed."

Zak grinned widely. Excellent! Things couldn't have worked out better.

The room was buzzing as the assembled agents began to file out.

Zak was almost at the door when the Colonel's voice stopped him in his tracks. "Agent Quicksilver," he barked. "You will report to my office immediately."

"Yes, Control," Zak replied. He had a nasty feeling he knew what the Colonel wanted to talk about.

It wasn't a conversation he was looking forward to.

Zak sat opposite Colonel Hunter, waiting for the thunder to roll and the lightning to strike. The Colonel was looking at him thoughtfully, his fingers tapping on his desk, his forehead furrowed.

The silence finally got too much.

"Why have I got an MI5 file?" Zak blurted. "Bug said it was opened straight after I was born."

"The file is classified Top Secret," the Colonel said, his voice slow and quiet. "I can't show it to you."

"Do you know what's inside it?" Zak asked.

"I know some details," said the Colonel. "The file was opened following the suspicious crash of a light aircraft in Canada." He paused, his fingers rattling on the desk. "I'm going to tell you all the truth I can, and you're going to have to find a way to deal with it. Do you understand?"

Zak nodded, a sick, heavy feeling building up in his stomach. What was he about to be told?

"The aircraft was a Cessna 206 Stationair, and had two people aboard. The pilot's name was John Trent. He was forty-one years old, a well-respected computer analyst. With him on the aircraft was his wife, Janet. She was thirty-eight." There was another long pause. "Thirteen weeks previously, Janet Trent had given birth to a boy. Mrs Trent was a field agent for British Intelligence." The Colonel glanced at Zak. "I'm not at liberty to tell you what department of MI5 she worked in, that information is classified at Ministerial level. All I can say is that she was an expert in her field. Are you following me?"

Zak swallowed hard. "Yes."

"The aeroplane was lost while Janet Trent was on a

top priority mission," the Colonel continued. "Because of the nature of her mission, MI5 treated the crash as suspicious. And because she was an employee of British Intelligence, a file was opened on her newborn son, the thinking being that if Mrs Trent's plane had been deliberately brought down, her immediate family may also be at risk."

"How long ago was this?" Zak croaked, but he had the horrible feeling he already knew the answer to that question.

"I think you can tell me that," said the Colonel.

"Fourteen years?" Zak said, strangely aware that his hands were shaking violently. "They . . ." His mouth was full of cotton wool. "They were my parents . . . ?"

"They were," said the Colonel.

The next question was somehow even harder to ask – it threw up so many conflicting emotions Zak could hardly bring himself to say the words. "Was my mother's codename Slingshot?"

Colonel Hunter gazed levelly at him. "No, it was not." The Colonel's eyes looked into his, as grey as the steel doors of a security vault. Unreadable. Hiding a thousand secrets.

"Is that true?" Zak whispered.

"I can't tell you everything, Zak," said the Colonel, and

Zak was struck by the fact that he used his real name for once. "But I promise I will never lie to you." He leaned back, his face relaxing. "You've done very well, Agent. I'm more than satisfied with your progress so far. Now – go and pack some things for your holiday. Enjoy yourself. You deserve it."

Zak gazed at him. "And Slingshot?" he asked hesitantly. "Who is Slingshot? Bug said you classified Slingshot's file the same day that I joined. Why did you do that?"

The Colonel stood up. "You're dismissed, Quicksilver," he said sharply. "Your seventy-two-hour leave begins in one hour and thirty-two minutes – I suggest you make the most of it."

"Thanks." Zak stood up and walked to the door. The Colonel had moved to a side desk and was already busy at a laptop.

Meeting over.

Zak sat next to Prince Viktor as the aeroplane soared above the Pyrenees. Neither of them was feeling very chatty. Zak spent most of the time gazing out of the window while the Prince thumbed listlessly through a gaming magazine, apparently reading the same articles over and over again. It was hardly surprising that they should be subdued and distracted. They both had a lot of tricky stuff to try and process.

Zak wished he could talk to his new friend about some of the things he'd learned from Colonel Hunter. But he couldn't – it was against Project 17 protocol to discuss that kind of thing with outsiders. Well, Zak made an exception to that rule with his old pal Dodge, the poetry-reciting down-and-out who lived in a packing crate under the arches of Waterloo station. It might sound weird to anyone else, but Zak and Dodge had been close friends for several years – and Zak would have trusted Dodge with his life.

Zak felt bad he hadn't been to see his old friend for so long – Project 17 training really cut into a person's free time. Dodge would have been exactly the person to tell about John and Janet Trent.

He could almost hear Dodge's creaky voice in his head.

So, what does it feel like to know these new things about your parents, Zachary?

Dodge was the only person who called him Zachary.

"I don't know, Dodge. It's as if the Colonel was talking about someone else's life. It didn't seem real."

Does it upset you to know they're dead?

"I guess so . . . kind of . . ."

And the fact that your mother was in MI5?

Zak gazed out of the window. He had no idea how he would have answered that question. He didn't have the faintest clue how he felt about that.

Somehow, the whole thing about his parents just made him, well . . . numb.

Maybe in time he'd feel . . . *something*. Glad or sad or intrigued or upset. But right now there was nothing.

Except for the fact that Colonel Hunter had refused to talk about Slingshot.

And at some stage, Zak was determined to get to the bottom of that particular mystery.

"Hey, Silver, what score did you reach by the end?" Zak lifted his head at the sound of Wildcat's voice, tilting his sunglasses down to look at her.

"Four thousand, seven hundred and twenty-eight," he said. "Including five hundred bonus points for taking down that hunter guy who was trying to shoot the Gallimimus." He lay back again on the sundeck of the royal yacht, stretching out luxuriously. On one side, Wildcat was sprawled on her front in a wide black hat, reading a book. On the other, Switch lay basking in the sunshine, eyes closed, plugged into his iPod.

The TR3000 had been everything the publicity had promised. Zak had never experienced anything like it. It really had been as if he was back in Jurassic times. He'd touched a Stegosaurus – and it had really felt the way a Stegosaurus ought to feel. And he'd been chased by a raptor. And he'd watched pterodactyls flying overhead, and Brachiosaurs wallowing in swamps and a Protoceratops protecting her eggs, along with a whole prehistoric world full of other amazing things that he would never forget. He could have gone on playing the incredible game all day. He was hoping for another chance later today, in fact.

Meanwhile, the sun was high in the crystal blue sky and seagulls swooped and called as the yacht bobbed on the clear Mediterranean waters. Zak turned a lazy eye landwards, gazing contentedly at the marinas and the colourful old-town buildings, and at the modern tower blocks beyond. His eyes lifted to the forested hills – and finally came to rest on the gothic towers of the Royal Palace.

This was the way to enjoy Montevisto – from the deck of a luxury yacht with no one to protect, no mission to fulfill, no evil terrorists to track down – just iced drinks and sunshine and a warm sea breeze.

Sheer bliss!

Bare feet padded across the deck. "Your phone was ringing," said Viktor. "I brought it up – I thought it might be something important."

"Oh, thanks." Zak sat up and took the Mob. He didn't bother mentioning to the Prince that he'd left it below decks so he wouldn't hear it if it rang. The very last thing he needed was a call from Fortress.

The chime was Colonel Hunter's dedicated tone.

Zak touched the screen, his heart sinking a little. "Yes, Control?"

"You'll be cutting your holiday one day short, Quicksilver," came the Colonel's brisk voice. "A place has opened up for you at the Academy. You start your sixteen-week course tomorrow at zero eight hundred hours. A return flight has been booked for you this evening. That's all." There was a soft click as Colonel Hunter disconnected the line.

"Oh," said Zak, deadpan. "Thank you, Control. I'm so happy about that."

"Not good news?" asked Viktor, looking at Zak's dejected expression.

"I have to go back early," sighed Zak. "There's a course I have to take."

Switch unplugged himself. "You knew it was coming," he said with a grin. "Look on the bright side, Silver – get through the course successfully and you'll be a fully fledged member of Project 17."

Yes, Switch was right. This was a good thing. It was what Zak wanted more than anything. All the same, it would have been nice to laze about here for a while longer, soaking up the sun and playing TR3000.

He stood up.

"Do you have to go back right now?" asked Viktor.

"No," Zak said with a smile. "There's something I'm definitely going to do first."

The Prince blinked at him. "What?"

"This!" Zak sprinted for the side of the yacht. He launched himself into the air, curving his body, his arms stretched on either side of his head, his fingers pointing the way as he dived smoothly and almost without a splash into the warm Mediterranean water.

Turn the page for a sneak preview of Zak Archer's next mission:

Burning Sky

CHAPTER **ONE**

NEW YORK. 21:30 LOCAL TIME.

Zak Archer twisted on the broad leather seat of the Lincoln MKZ and gave a final wave to the cheering crowds as the limousine slid away from the concert hall and nosed smoothly into the traffic of West 57th Street in New York.

He watched the lights of Carnegie Hall disappear into the distance. It was late evening, but the bright lights of the big city shone all around them and the noise of the traffic was loud and constant. New York never slept, and Zak felt as though the spirit of the city had got right inside him. He was wide awake and wired as they glided between the tall buildings. So far Operation Mozart was right on target.

The autograph-hunting crowd at the stage door hadn't noticed that the boy handing out signed CDs through the open window of the limo was not the same one who had wowed them at the concert grand piano only fifteen minutes earlier. The switch had gone perfectly.

Zak grinned as he settled back into the plush leather and loosened his bowtie. A huge bunch of red roses lay at his side, the cellophane wrap crackling. A few remaining CDs were scattered on the seat. He picked one of them up.

The front of the booklet showed a boy of about fourteen, dressed very formally in white tie and tailcoat, with a slightly dreamy, faraway look in the brown eyes that gazed out from behind black-rimmed glasses.

Zak read the fancy lettering. *Alexi Roman Plays Selections from the Classics.* He could see his own reflection in the background of the CD cover. He smiled again and pushed up the black-rimmed glasses that had slid down his own nose.

They were clear glass. Zak had perfect vision. The spectacles were just part of the disguise. Along with the nerdy hairstyle and the uncomfortable tuxedo he was wearing. Jeans and a sloppy T-shirt were more Zak's style.

Zak stared at his ghostly reflection alongside Alexi's picture.

"Weird," he said, not for the first time. He still couldn't get over how alike they looked. Zak Archer and Alexi Roman – with just a bad haircut and glasses to help with the illusion, Zak was the boy genius' identical twin!

Which was exactly why Zak had been called in to play the lead role in Project 17's operation.

The limousine came to a sudden juddering halt. Zak peered through the glass divide that separated him from the driver and out through the windscreen. A bunch of over-excited people were running across the road, disrupting the traffic, laughing and yelling.

The intercom crackled. "Sorry, Mr Roman," came the chauffeur's voice. "It looks like someone's been celebrating a bit too heartily."

"No problem," Zak replied, impersonating Alexi's slightly posh voice. Colonel Hunter had warned him to speak as little as possible, but Zak liked showing off how well he could imitate Alexi's way of talking.

The drunken group wandered off and the traffic started moving again. A couple of turns and a few long straight streets later they approached the tall oblong of golden lights that formed the front of the Waites Hotel.

The chauffeur spun the wheel and the limousine swung off the main street and cruised towards the sloping road that would take them to the private car park under the hotel.

Zak took his Project 17 issue smartphone out of his pocket. It was a slim silvery oval, cutting-edge touch-screen tech, known among the agents as a Mob. He was about to tap out *arrived Waites safely* when he was blinded by a ferocious blast of red light. It was as if the sun had exploded in his face. Almost instantaneously there came a huge erupting roar and a flash of heat and force. It lifted the limousine off the road and sent it spinning end over end through the flaming air.

20 HOURS EARLIER, THE SAME DAY.
UK TIME 06:30.
Dateline: Fortress.

It was only the lack of windows that suggested there was anything strange about the room, but in fact there was one thing in particular that made this room very unusual indeed. It was thirty metres under the ground, at the heart of the sprawling subterranean complex known as Fortress – headquarters of the specialist branch of

British Intelligence called Project 17.

Great heavy steel girders spanned the ceiling. Halogen lights bathed the white walls and lit up the rows of tables and chairs that faced a huge plasma screen, which was flickering at one end.

The steel girders supported the weight of five metres of reinforced concrete. Another twenty-five metres above the room, the streets of London teemed with life – and only a handful of the seven and a half million people who lived and worked in the city had the slightest inkling of the things that went on far, far below their bustling feet.

Colonel Hunter stood to one side of the plasma screen. Called 'Control' by his agents, he ran the whole of Project 17. He was tall and gaunt with grey hair, a ramrod-straight back and piercing grey eyes that looked as if they could drill through sheet steel. Facing him from behind the desks were Zak and a group of his fellow agents.

They were being briefed on a new mission.

Operation Mozart.

Zak was still a bit bleary-eyed – he'd been wrenched from a deep sleep by an agent named Switchblade, who had grabbed him by the shoulders and yelled in his ear. "Rise and Shine, Silver! Control wants us in the briefing room. Right now." Switch was a big, blond, blue-eyed boy a couple of years older than Zak. A good person to have with you in a tight fix, as Zak had already learned.

Zak had scrambled out of bed and thrown on some clothes. His bedside clock showed 06:12. But these early rises were just one small part of the craziness that came from being on Colonel Hunter's team. And a new mission would mean a welcome diversion from Project 17's schoolroom. Only agents with missions were allowed to skip lessons.

When he had joined Project 17, Zak had been given the codename Quicksilver, but most of the others just called him Silver. Birth names were never used. He had no idea of Switchblade's real name – nor the real identities or backgrounds of any of the other young agents who sat around him in the briefing room. You didn't ask. When someone joined Project 17, a door was closed on their previous life and family. Closed and locked.

At the time, Zak hadn't even known he had a family to lock out. As far as he'd been aware, he'd been orphaned as a baby; and he'd assumed the rest of his life could be found in his Social Services file. There were some foster parents that hadn't worked out, followed by four years in a children's home. The only part of his life that he felt belonged entirely to him was his friendship with his pal Dodge.

Zak had first encountered Dodge on Waterloo Bridge, two or three years ago. The man was obviously homeless, and Zak had taken pity on him – it was winter and he'd looked cold and hungry. Zak had offered him half a sandwich. They had started chatting, and Zak had been surprised at how well spoken the man was. He kept quoting from poems and stuff like that, which was odd and intriguing. But what Zak had liked straight away about Dodge was the fact that he listened to what Zak had to say. In Zak's experience, that was pretty unusual in an adult.

They'd quickly become friends. Dodge was the only person Zak had told about Project 17. He knew strictly speaking that he shouldn't have told *anyone* – but Dodge had sworn never to repeat anything Zak told him. And Zak trusted Dodge without reservation.

Everything had changed for Zak shortly after joining Project 17. He'd learned that his mother had been an MI5 field agent and that she and his father had been killed in suspicious circumstances three months after he'd been born, while they were on a mission in Canada. And if that wasn't enough to fry his brain, he'd also been told he was the subject of a top secret MI5 file, opened at the time of his birth.

He had the feeling there were a lot more secrets to be unearthed – especially the truth behind the mysterious MI5 agent with the codename Slingshot. Colonel Hunter had said that Slingshot was not his mother – but Zak wasn't so sure, and one day he'd vowed he'd get to the bottom of the mystery.

"Watch this webcam video," Hunter told them. "I'll explain what it means afterwards."

He pressed a remote control and the flickering on the plasma screen resolved itself into an alarming picture. A man's face filled the screen, sweaty and panicking, hugely enlarged, so that every bead of moisture stood out clearly on his forehead and upper lip. As far as Zak could make out, the background was an ordinary, featureless room.

The man had pale, waxy skin and his greying hair was a mess. There were heavy black rings under his puffy, bloodshot eyes. He was hunched over the webcam, his eyes wide, his mouth twisting into a grimace as he spoke.

"Peter," the man gasped. "I'm so sorry . . . they forced me . . . I had to do what they said . . . I had no choice." His eyes darted to the side as though he had heard something sinister. He leaned closer, his fear plainly showing. "I know we haven't seen one another for a long time, but you're the one person I can trust with this. And I know you can do what needs to be done." Again the anxious eyes flickered to one side. "There's going to be a terrorist attack – you have to prevent it."

Zak thought he heard a distant bang, like a door being kicked open.

"The details are in the post to you – but don't try to open it without the key." The man's head snapped around and he got up suddenly so that a filthy and torn shirt filled the screen. His voice was quieter now that he was further from the microphone, but his words were perfectly clear. "Be careful, Peter. You'll destroy it if you try to get in without the key."

A different voice shouted something in the background.

The man bent forwards and his face came back into view. "Protect the boy, Peter . . . you must protect him . . . he's the only one who. . ." The man's voice cut short with a cry. The image swung and tipped over. The screen went blank.

There were a few moments of silence in the briefing room.

Zak was the first to speak. "What was that all about? Who was he?"

"The man's name is Stephen Avon," Colonel Hunter replied.

"The missing electronics genius?" exclaimed Wildcat, an ash-blonde Goth girl agent. She narrowed her sooty black eyes. "Wow – I'd hardly have recognized him. He looks a total wreck and he's lost a lot of weight since his picture was in the news."

Colonel Hunter pressed the remote and a slideshow of newspaper front pages rolled across the screen. The headlines were all variations on: *TOP BOFFIN MISSING* or *ELECTRONICS EXPERT WITH MI5 CONNECTIONS DISAPPEARS.*

The static images changed to a television news report. A well-groomed female newsreader was speaking. There was a photo of a smiling and well-fed Stephen Avon on screen at her back.

"Speculation is growing that Dr Stephen Avon, who went missing from his Berkshire home five days ago, may have been in the pay of a foreign power. Fears have risen about Dr Avon's loyalties since it was revealed by MI5 sources that the laboratory where he worked, and where he kept all the files relevant to his experiments in the field of electro-magnetics, was destroyed in a fire on the night of his disappearance."

Colonel Hunter muted the sound. The newsreader's

larger-than-life mouth continued to open and close silently at his side.

"Dr Avon has been missing for five months now," said the Colonel. "An extensive international investigation into his whereabouts is still underway, but there have been no new developments for some time." He frowned. "There are three possible explanations of what may have happened to him. One: he defected and took all his research with him. Two: he was abducted. And three: he had some kind of mental breakdown. I think this video makes it quite clear that it was option two."

"When did you get the video, Control?" asked Jackhammer, a hefty square-jawed boy with slick brown hair.

"It arrived just after midnight," said Colonel Hunter.

A small, round-faced boy with big eyes and a deep fringe spoke. "It didn't come through me, Control," he said. "I'd have got an alert."

"I received it on my home laptop, Bug," said the Colonel.

Bug was Project 17's slightly odd über-nerd. All things electronic went through him as he sat alone in his little office with its multiple plasma screens and cutting-edge computer technology.

"He sent it to you personally, Control?" asked Wildcat. "Why would he do that?"

The Colonel's sharp eyes scanned the faces in front of him. "I shared a room with Dr Avon at university many years ago," he said. "We were close friends once, although our careers sent us in different directions once we left university." His eyes glittered. "I knew of his work, of course," he continued. "But when the news broke of his disappearance, I hadn't seen him for fifteen years or more."

Something clicked in Zak's mind. Colonel Hunter's first name must be Peter – that was the name Dr Avon had used. Peter Hunter. It was quite strange to learn that the Colonel even *had* a first name.

"Send the video through to my office, Control," said Bug. "It'll take me five minutes to work out where it came from."

Colonel Hunter gave Bug the ghost of a smile. "I already know, Bug," he said. "I did a trace. It was sent from an internet motel in Palmetto Bay, Miami."

"So Dr Avon was in America all the time?" said Wildcat. "How weird is that?"

"I made contact with the FBI as soon as I saw the video," Colonel Hunter said. "They didn't know he was there. FBI Special Agents were sent to the address. The room had been hired for the day by a man going by the name of Spencer Arnold. He paid in cash. No luggage. The motel room was empty and there were signs of a disturbance, including the fact that the motel room's internet computer was broken."

"For Spencer Arnold, read Stephen Avon," said Wildcat. "Who was he scared of, Control? Who was after him?"

"Whoever it was, I think they got him," said Jackhammer under his breath.

Even though it had been a major scandal, Zak only vaguely remembered the news about Dr Avon disappearing. Back then, that kind of thing wouldn't have interested him. Now he was intrigued.

"What kind of work was Dr Avon doing when he went missing?" Zak asked.

"He was working for a research branch of the Ministry of Defence," the Colonel replied. "He was brilliant at university. Streets ahead of everyone else." The Colonel's face grew even graver. "Shortly before his disappearance, I heard that he was involved in pioneering research on electro-magnetic pulses. Pioneering work. He was close to a major breakthrough, I believe."

Zak had never even heard of electro-magnetic pulses.

"EMPs?" said a small, slender girl behind him. "They're supposed to be able to knock out everything electronic within the pulse zone – but I thought it was only theoretical." Zak turned to look at her. Her codename was Moonbeam. She had huge green eyes and flaming red hair that framed her pale, freckled face. Zak had only met her a couple of times. She'd been away on some special training course for several months. "Did Dr Avon work out how to use an EMP as a weapon, Control?" she asked. "Is that what this is all about?"

"He was certainly researching the military capabilities of the EMP," growled Colonel Hunter.

"What would an EMP weapon do?" asked Zak.

Switchblade turned to him. "If you detonated an EMP bomb, everything electrical within a twenty kilometre radius would be fried," he said. "Everything! Every computer, every electrical circuit, all hospital equipment, electronic files and data – the power grid – it would all be gone. Finished. Finito!"

"If an EMP were set off over London it would cause total chaos," added Moonbeam. "The banks wouldn't be able to function, which would mean there would be no money available for *anything.* Any aeroplanes in the sky would be brought down. Mobile phones would be dead. Traffic lights would all be down. Trains wouldn't run. Electric lighting would be non-existent. The whole city would be a criminal free-for-all, and there would be nothing the Government or the police could do about it."

Zak was still trying to take in the enormity of this when Colonel Hunter began to speak. "It's clear now that Stephen Avon was kidnapped, either by a rogue foreign government, or by a terrorist organization. The fact that Dr Avon tried to warn us of a terrorist attack only confirms this." He looked at Moonbeam. "Clearly, he managed to escape from wherever he was being kept, but as you saw from the video, his captors caught up with him again."

Zak could see how that made sense. Dr Avon had obviously been terrified in the video. Someone had crashed in on him right in the middle of the webcam recording.

"Dr Avon referred to a boy," said Switchblade. "Do you know who he was talking about, Control?"

"Yes, I do," said Colonel Hunter. He turned back to the screen and clicked the remote.

A photo came up on screen. It was of a boy. Zak guessed he was probably about fourteen – Zak's own age. He was sitting on a stool facing a grand piano. He had short black hair that didn't look as if it had ever been anywhere near a decent hairdresser or any styling gel. He was wearing horrible black-rimmed glasses and an old-fashioned polo-neck jumper. He had a wistful, faraway look in his brown eyes, as though he was off in his own little world.

Zak was slightly puzzled by a number of sharply indrawn breaths around him. Jackhammer gave a stifled snort of laughter and Switch murmured a soft, "*Wow – talk about snap!*"

"This is Alexi Roman," said Hunter. "Dr Avon was with him about an hour before he made contact with me. I believe this must be the boy Stephen Avon was referring to in his message."

"And if Dr Avon said you needed to protect him, he must be in some kind of danger?" said Switchblade, glancing curiously at Zak from the corner of his eye. "Something to do with the terrorist attack?"

Why was everyone being so weird suddenly?

"I think that's a reasonable expectation," said the Colonel. "Fortunately, we're in the perfect position to keep Alexi Roman from harm." His eyes fixed on Zak. "We can supply a very convincing substitute."

The faces of all the other agents also turned to Zak.

"What?" asked Zak, starting to feel uncomfortable. "What's everyone looking at me for?"

Wildcat stared at him. "You're kidding?" she said. "Don't you see it?" She gestured towards the screen.

"You're the spitting image of him, Silver!"

Zak stared at the enlarged photo of the geeky boy then back at Wildcat, aghast.

"I am not!" he gasped.

Switch poked him in the ribs. "Trust me, some black hair dye, a bad haircut and some truly horrible glasses and you're *him*!"

"And you're booked on a flight to New York this afternoon, Quicksilver," said Colonel Hunter. "This time tomorrow, you're going to *be* Alexi Roman."

ACCESS
ALL AREAS
Visit
www.codenamequicksilver.com
for